GOOD-BYE, SON
AND OTHER STORIES

Books by Janet Lewis

GOOD-BYE, SON AND OTHER STORIES

AGAINST A DARKENING SKY

THE WIFE OF MARTIN GUERRE

THE INVASION

Good-bye, SON

AND OTHER STORIES

By JANET LEWIS

Swallow Press/Ohio University Press

Athens, Ohio   London

© Copyright, 1943, 1946 by Janet Lewis Winters
Originally published by Doubleday & Company, Inc.,
Garden City, New York

Revised edition published 1986
Swallow Press books are published by
Ohio University Press

Library of Congress Cataloging-in-Publication Data

Lewis, Janet, 1899-
  Good-bye, son, and other stories.

  I. Title.
PS3523.E866G6   1986   813'.52   85-27731
ISBN 0-8040-0867-1
ISBN 0-8040-0868-X (pbk.)

For
HERBERT *and* KATHERINE

Contents

~~~~~~

PROSERPINA   11

RIVER   24

SUMMER PARTIES   32

NELL   41

THE HOUSE   50

LITTLE HELLCAT   63

SUNDAY DINNER   68

WITH THE SPRING   80

APRICOT HARVEST   91

PEOPLE DON'T WANT US   104

PICNIC, 1943   128

GOOD-BYE, SON   144

THE BREAKABLE CUP   203

GOOD-BYE, SON
AND OTHER STORIES

Proserpina

~~~~~~

*H*E STOOD looking down at the casket with its blue velvet casing, its inner lining of puffed white satin, and its rows of silver handles.

"Haven't you anything more—ah—more dignified? A little plainer and more dignified?" he said.

His coat was unbuttoned, showing the vest and the gold watch chain with its dangling seals and trophies. His hands were in his trousers pockets, and his straw hat was shoved far back on his head. He glanced at the mortician with an oddly worried, humorous look; and the mortician, a young man with a red, freckled face, wearing a brown-and-white checked suit of an unbecoming shade, led him to the other side of the room and indicated a simpler casket finished in gray velvet.

"This is real dignified," said the mortician. "It's quite a bit cheaper, too; as a matter of fact, seventy-five bucks less. We sell a good many of this model," he added.

"Can't say it appeals to me awfully," said the customer.

"Well, now, you don't expect any of 'em to do that

exactly, do you?" said the mortician with a macabre grin.

"Don't get funny," said the customer.

"Well, now, Johnnie," said the mortician, "I'll show you everything we've got, but I bet you take the gray one in the end."

They continued their tour of the big room, Johnnie whistling softly, as the mortician, tapping with his pencil, explained the virtues and values of his various models. Johnnie's eyes retained their expression of semihumorous concern, but by and by he stopped whistling and said with resignation, "You win. Gimme the gray one and I'll write you a check for it."

They went into the next room, which was the reception room, their feet making no sound on the heavily carpeted floor. Johnnie sat down in an upholstered mahogany chair and began to write out a check, holding the book on his knee.

A diluted sunshine fell through the tan silk curtains. A fern in a wicker flower stand in the corner of the room was growing quietly, exhaling the freshness of its slight breath upon the air; and on the walls were small pictures in narrow gold frames, depicting spring woods at evening, heathery hills, a thatched cottage, sheep coming home along a country road, the colors and the compositions all properly subdued and quiet. The mortician took the check which Johnnie held out to him and waved it slowly up and down to dry it.

"Thanks," he said. "I'll hold it for you. But say, what's struck you, pickin' it out so young? You look as if you'd last forever. You're not contemplating self-destruction by any chance?"

"I should say not," said Johnnie. He leaned back in

the chair and crossed his legs, his right ankle resting on his left knee. "I was around to see my doctor, just for a general look-over before I get settled at the island for the winter. And he says to me, 'Johnnie, my boy, how often do I have to tell you that you'd better get your affairs fixed up while there's time? You may last twenty years,' he says, 'or you may pop off tonight. Go and get your affairs straightened out, and then amuse yourself in peace.'"

"Heart?" interpolated the mortician.

"Yeah. So I overhauled my will and what not, and then, seein' as there's nobody else to do this little job for me, I thought I'd better do it myself. Selah. I never felt spryer."

He got up and, buttoning his coat, made for the door. The mortician opened it for him.

"So long, Johnnie," he said innocently. "See you again."

"Probably," said Johnnie dryly, "but not too soon, my boy, not too soon."

The street was bright but empty. Johnnie drew a deep breath, feeling as if he had emerged from underground. What fine brisk air! He took his hat off, put it on straight, thrust his hands into his coat pockets, and proceeded past the small clean residences, each with its mowed green lawn, to the end of the block. Here he turned into a business street where there were people, autos, an occasional streetcar, and store windows. Autumnal clarity was over everything, enriched by the noonday sunshine. Above the rattle of a streetcar, when it passed, he heard the deep tooting of a freighter drawing up to the locks and shriller tootings from the tugs which convoyed it.

He liked the noises of the Soo. He passed an Indian leaning against a barbershop window, and a candy kitchen
from which issued a group of high school girls in short,
sleeveless dresses, tight little tams on their heads. A little
farther down the street he stopped at a restaurant, and,
entering, hung his hat on a peg and sat down at a table
near the window. A girl offered him the menu, written
with indelible pencil on a piece of white paper, and he
said without reading it, "Broiled whitefish and blueberry
pie. And coffee."

A white muslin curtain, very clean and fresh, pro-
tected the lower part of the window from the inspection
of the street. Above that, on the glass, in letters now
backward, he deciphered FOUNTAIN LUNCH AND RES-
TAURANT. He looked about the room and watched with
amusement, for a few minutes, a boy hunched over the
counter at the Fountain Lunch ogling the girl who
waited on him. The recent transaction at the mortician's
had given Johnnie a queer, uneasy feeling. He shook his
head slightly and drummed on the table with his finger
tips. He was a short, plump man with blue eyes and
white hair, which was parted down the middle of his
head and cut close at the sides. His nose was blunt and
his upper lip long and smooth-shaven. The stubble of his
beard, unless he had just shaved, gave his pink cheeks
a frosty, rimy look.

The whitefish was very good, and so was the blueberry
pie. He ate slowly, enjoying himself deliberately, but the
idea of the mortician and of his purchase persisted.

"I shouldn't have done that," he said to himself. "No
sir, it was a mistake—too much like asking for something
that you don't want." He took a sip of coffee and said,

"Well, it's the last time I do anything like that. Next time I'll leave it to the other fellow." He chuckled at his joke.

The girl who came to clear the table paused a minute. "How's everything down at the island, Mr. Plows?"

"Fine," he said, "just fine."

He had more than enough time in which to walk down to the Johnstone Slip and catch the *Neon*, which would take him home. He went around to the stationer's and bought himself some magazines. The boy who waited on him said, "Nice day, Mr. Plows. How's everything down at the island?"

"Fine and dandy," said Johnnie.

A couple of young men were standing before a hardware store window inspecting the hunting apparatus on view there. Johnnie stood with them for a few minutes, but the stuffed head of a moose regarded him with a glassy eye above the Winchesters and game bags, and he wandered on. He stopped in front of a jeweler's, a little place with only one show window. An array of gaily enameled cigarette lighters pleased him, and he said to himself, "Why don't you get one, Johnnie? Be a sport, you're only young once. Treat yourself."

He bought a blue one and then walked down to the river. The *Neon* lay in the slip along with a small fast boat of the United States Coast Guard service. She was a fairly large launch with a closed-in engine room and a covered deck at the stern. Her owner, who was also chief mate and engineer, was sitting on a barrel on the wharf in the shade of the warehouses. He hopped off as Johnnie approached and greeted him.

"Have a nice day?" he said.

"First rate," said Johnnie. "When do we go?"

"Oh, any time the mail comes. I guess there's nobody else coming down with us."

"Well, let's climb on board and have a smoke," said Johnnie. "I brought you some funny pictures."

A coolness rose from the water, sharply pleasant in the warmth of the air. The surface of the water was sprinkled with a sooty dust, with chips and straws, and undulated slightly. The young man seated himself in a camp chair, leaning against the cabin wall and bracing his feet against the railing. He was lean and dark, a French-Canadian type. He took the magazines which Johnnie offered him and spread them out lazily on his knee, meanwhile looking up the green hill toward the road, or at the blackened wooden walls of the slip, or at the sunlight on the deck.

Johnnie got out his lighter and lit his cigar with ostentation.

The boy said, "Pretty swell you're getting, Johnnie."

Johnnie smirked, capped the tiny flame, and put the instrument back in his pocket with a great air of ownership. The boy laughed. The mail came, and they started the engine and chugged out into the Straits.

The air freshened immediately. There was a good icy nip to it in spite of the sun. Freighters were coming up-stream, some with a tow, and freighters were starting downstream. The low, deep throbbing of their engines sounded across the water. A ferryboat was crossing from the Canadian Sault, and the Laurentians were blue. It was very beautiful, this scene of distant busyness, and as Johnnie looked at it, it drew him into a reverie in which it seemed that he would never again see these boats, this water, and that he should look at them well. When he awoke from this reverie his light had gone out. They were well down in Hay Lake, and the boy stood at the door of the cabin, propped inside the frame of it, where he could keep one hand on the tiller rope.

Johnnie looked ruefully at the end of his cigar, then, seeing his companion watching him, smiled, and drew the blue lighter from his pocket. The little flame blazed up, the rolled leaves of tobacco caught, and Johnnie smirked again as he put out the light. The boy grinned.

"That sure is swell, Johnnie. When you die, leave it to me, will you?"

"Take it now," said Johnnie imperatively. "Great snakes, I bought it for you anyway. It's a present. You're a friend of mine. Can't I buy you a present?"

The boy was pleased but apologetic. He took the blue lighter and fingered it lovingly from time to time, through the rest of the afternoon.

They reached Encampment at dark. The *Neon* let Johnnie off at the store, his store, and went on down-river to the post office. There was a light in the store, and another in the small kitchen behind it. As he approached the back door he caught a glimpse of Martha Waley, the woman who helped him with the store and kept house for him. She smiled at him over her shoulder as he came in.

"Hello, Johnnie," she said. "Have a nice day?" and, without waiting for an answer, "Sue Tolliver just came into the store. Go on and ask her what she wants. I got supper on the stove and I don't want to spoil it."

He put his hat and bundle of magazines on the kitchen table and went into the front room. Behind the counter stood the little Tolliver girl, her sweater buttoned high about her neck and her straight pale hair straggling down into her eyes.

Johnnie said, "Well, little lady, what can I give you?"

She consulted a small piece of crumpled paper and said, "Matches, soap, bacon."

"What kind of soap?" said Johnnie, setting a box of matches on the counter. It was cozy in the store with all the rows of breakfast foods, oatmeal, canned goods. A shelf of jams and pickles in glass jars behind Johnnie's back was particularly enticing. The oil lamp stood on the glass top of the candy counter. The child shook her head at the question.

"Kitchen soap," she suggested.

"I'll make it Lily White," said Johnnie. "That's the kind your ma generally gets. Here, now, don't go putting them things in your pockets. I'm going to wrap 'em up for you." The child put them back on the counter sheepishly.

"Lookit," he said. He stacked them deftly on the slab of bacon, unrolled a fair sheet of brown paper, wrapped everything, mitered the corners neatly, tied the package, spinning the string out of a wire cocoon hung overhead. "There," he said, shoving it toward her, "ain't that an elegant package? Anything else, little lady?"

She shook her head, smiling and mute, and edged out the door. Johnnie, also smiling, entered the purchases in a charge book and went back into the kitchen.

He did a pretty fair business in the summer, supplying the summer colony with canned goods and, now and then, fresh vegetables and fruit. In the winter there were only three other households. He dined out regularly every

Sunday with one or the other of them, played endless games of solitaire, and enjoyed the hermitage. He was proud of the store. It was little and bright; and built onto the kitchen in the rear he had a little glassed-in sun parlor with cretonne curtains and wicker chairs. It was so little that the kitchen stove heated it thoroughly even in the coldest weather. From the windows he could see the river, both upstream and down, for the store was on a point.

Beside the store, in a small thicket of Indian plum, stood a guesthouse, where his housekeeper lived. Johnnie himself bunked over the store. The guesthouse was hardly bigger than a sandwich wagon. It had been a Builders' and Roofers' float in a trade pageant at the Soo, and was such a good job that Johnnie had bought it, cheap, and set it up on a log foundation next to the store. He built a stairway of three steps leading up to the door, and there you were.

Martha Waley was in a good mood tonight. They had a pleasant supper, and after the dishes were washed he invited her to play a game of two-handed bridge with him. But she said she was tired and wanted to go to bed. She took the lamp from the store, and he saw its light moving over the leaves and low bushes. Then she entered the house, shut the door, and the light disappeared.

He read for a while and then got out the cards for a game of solitaire. The vague feeling of misfortune which he had downed successfully from the moment when he had parted from the blue lighter returned now, rather more potent than before.

"It was a damn fool thing to do," he argued. "Ask for trouble and you'll get it sure enough."

The cards were firm and smooth in his hands, and the little accurate flip and shuffle consoled him somewhat. He played the game through, his uneasiness deepening momently, but when he had gathered up the cards again, he sighed in disgust and gave himself up entirely to his gloom.

He thought of the coffin, thought of it minutely, thought of himself in it, he, Johnnie Plows, in his best suit, but without a hat, of course, lying in white satin. The image depressed him terribly, and there is no knowing how long he might have remained sunk in misery had not a grain of common sense come to his help.

"Shucks," he said, "this is all the wrong way to go about it, planning my material hereafter instead of my spiritual." He repeated it, "My spiritual hereafter." Then he sighed. "Yeah," he said, "but how do you work it?"

Phrases like "the remission of sins," "examine your conscience," "the way of the transgressor," "through the eye of a needle," came into his mind. His sins, as he remembered them, were all so long ago, when he was on the road, and "only the usual sins, anyway," he said, finding it hard to be interested in them. The face of his wife appeared to him dimly, patient and faintly lined, a face seen through a mist, one that he might encounter in his spiritual hereafter. As for Martha Waley, he'd had nothing to do with Martha Waley. People could talk if they wanted to; it didn't concern the problem in hand.

A clergyman, now, would know better how to go about it. But the last clergyman he remembered having talked with had been the circuit preacher, and they hadn't talked about sin or redemption either. Or death. He had stayed for a couple of weeks in the guesthouse before the days of Martha Waley, and they had gone fishing.

The face of the circuit preacher grew before his eyes, a long brown face with only a few wrinkles, but those deeply incised; his eyes gray and deep-set, his eyebrows gray and tufted.

"Looked like a Rail Splitter if there ever was one," said Johnnie.

They got up one morning at four o'clock in order to catch some bass for the judge. The judge had gone down to Chicago several weeks before, but his wife had stayed at the island with their little boy, who suffered from hay fever. It was the morning she was leaving, to rejoin the judge. They were going to send them down by her.

At four o'clock it was dark, and the river was the most curious cold expanse he'd ever laid eyes on. "That was when hot coffee tasted good," he said. As they pulled out from the dock they saw the Great Dipper stooping over Rains's barn. "Lookit," said Johnnie. "By golly, you could pitch hay into it."

The preacher smiled. "You've got a fancy, Johnnie," he said. "A fancy." They got the fish all right, a fine stringerful, but they barely made it back to the dock in time for the boat. That was before the *Elva* was taken off the run. There she lay, as they rowed up to the store. They were taking in the gangplank as Johnnie rushed out on the dock, waving his hands. The judge's wife looked aghast.

"But how can I travel with a stringerful of fish!"

"Oh," said Johnnie, "you just let the porter take care of them. Think of it! Black bass for breakfast in Chicago. I bet it tickles the judge. Here today and there tomorrow. No, I *ain't* quoting Scripture."

Captain Stewart leaned over the railing on the top deck.

"What's this I hear, Johnnie? Sending fish out of the state without a permit?"

"Just a snack for breakfast, Captain," said Johnnie.

The preacher hurried up with the fish then, and the last Johnnie had seen of the judge's wife that year she was standing on the lower deck of the *Elva* in her city clothes, wiping her eyes with one hand and holding a string of wet fish with the other.

He missed the preacher after he left.

Then, for no reason, he remembered a very hot spring day when he was going for green onions and lettuce to Miss Hallie Rains's. On the American side of the river the woods were wet and cold, drifts of snow still lying underneath the bushes, but on the sandy road which skirted the Canadian shore the sun was hot as if through a burning glass. He walked along the road carrying his coat, taking off his hat now and again to mop his forehead. The sunlight entered his bones, making them feel awake and limber. A fat old man, he was, feeling limber. He said to himself, "If I was a seed I'd sprout."

On the gate to the Rains farm it said "Sea Gull Ontario Post Office." He went around to the back yard without meeting anyone. Half a dozen white ducks with orange feet were walking about in front of the milk shed.

He heard the voices of men farther up the hill in the fields, and the voice of a woman in the kitchen, probably that of Miss Hallie. He crossed the kitchen porch that was low, almost on a level with the ground, and tapped at the screen door, his basket on his arm.

Miss Hallie made him go into the front room, while

she set his basket on the kitchen table. She had been talking with her sister, Mrs. Eddie Smith, who nodded at him pleasantly and went outdoors, humming. The front room was papered with a green satin stripe, light green, dark green, and hung with crayon portraits of the family. There was a small organ. The portiere between it and the next room was made of strings of wooden beads all hanging straight and parallel to the floor, and giving the illusion of a material. Miss Hallie came in with a glass of dandelion wine and a piece of cake, warm from the oven, on a white dish. She was glad to see him. He told her all the news from the other shore as he sipped his wine. It was fine, delicately fine, and cold. A breeze from the kitchen swung the bead portiere, which rattled lightly. And there was Miss Hallie looking at him, her eyes brown and kind behind the thick lenses of her spectacles. There she was.

River

~~~~~~

*I*N THE SHALLOWS the boat grounded, and it began to rain again. The children lifted their faces and sniffed the dampness, and Scotty put on his rubber cap that made him look like a devil. The Dominie stepped overboard with his shoes on and took the narrow painter over his shoulder. The boat lifted, floating lightly. Edith wanted to get out and push; she took her sandals off. But the twins wouldn't let her.

"It's probably over your head," said Scott.

Edith said, "Pooh."

The boat slipped through the rushes, the round green stems bent and rose behind them unharmed in a wall. They scraped softly against the sides of the boat, making a prolonged, firm "hush." The rain thickened, and the Dominie's back under the yellow poncho looked very high and large.

When the rushes ended and they came to the deep place between the rushes and the shore, the Dominie stepped back into the boat, which rocked under him, sending long ripples in arcs all over the still water. The rain seemed to stop. He took an oar and paddled to the exact center of the pool, dropped the small muddy anchor, and sat down.

They baited their hooks and the Dominie set the minnow bucket under the thwart. "To keep the sun off it," he said. The twins smiled.

Edith listened to the quiet. It was made up of little noises. There was the clicking of the reels as they all let out their lines and hunted for bottom, and reeled in a little. There was Scotty talking to his minnow, which he had dropped twice and was still working over. There was the water lipping the bottom of the boat. It was not cold, but it was very wet. Scott finally hooked his minnow, holding the little cold body carefully in his left hand and passing the point of the blue steel hook under the chin and up through the nose. The minnow did not wink or quiver, and when he dropped it overboard it gave a little flip with its tail and swam down out of sight.

"You've got a bite," said Edith.

"Weed," said John, reeling in.

The weed was a bright shiny green. It was twined about the hook and the minnow was about three inches above it on the line. John detached the minnow and threw it away with a wide sweep of his arm. They heard it splash, and then, almost immediately, another splash as a gull swooped for it and got it. The Dominie passed the minnow bucket without comment. The gull was a little Napoleon with bright red feet and a body the color of the cloudy sky.

The Dominie filled his pipe, tamping the tobacco with the tip of his little finger, and lighted it. When he bent his head to shield the match some water on the brim of his hat rolled off in round drops. His glasses were dry, but his brown beard and mustachios were dewed with wet.

Edith said, "There goes the *Elva*."

The boys lifted their eyes from their lines and watched the small white boat steaming far down-channel, its straight prow lifted and the two decks slanting backward as if to shed the rain. The shore was near them, rushes, tag alder, and Indian plum. Now in late June the leaves were summer foliage, thick and dark. There was a long pile of pulpwood on the beach, cut during the winter and waiting for some schooner like the *Our Son* to take it on downstream. They knew that it was five o'clock because of the *Elva*.

The rain began again and settled to a quiet steady downpour. Scott began to sing.

"Shut up," said John cheerfully, "you'll scare the fish."

"Sounds in the air don't scare the fish," said Scotty. "It's your big feet. Not right, sir?"

"Perfectly right," said the Dominie. Scott went on singing and the others joined. They sang, "Oh, the ocean waves may roll," and the raindrops, hitting the water on all sides of them, sounded like dried peas thrown on leather. Edith put out her tongue and began to lick the rain from the corners of her cheeks.

The Dominie looked at his wet children and they smiled back at him. They could hardly be any wetter, he thought, but they looked healthy enough. Even the pallor of the little girl had a healthy brightness. Her hair held the water from her head except near her face and the back of her neck where the locks were pasted to the skin. The Dominie took his pipe from between his teeth to say, "Her hair hung down upon her face Like seaweed on a clam."

They did not catch a single fish.

It was a good deal after six when they passed through the reeds again and regained the open river. The sky was a great pearly dome, reflected on the water whitely, and the shores were dark. The rain had stopped at last, the water was smooth. Edith sat in the prow because she weighed the least, where she looked over the Dominie's back at the two boys and, beyond them, at the American shore. They were heading for Canada.

"Why didn't they bite?" said Scott. "Wasn't the water cold enough? I hate to be skunked."

"Probably too early in the season," said John. "They haven't had time to grow up yet."

"Oh, you," said Scott. "We didn't catch them *all*, last year." He added, to the Dominie, "Deadhead ahead on your right, sir."

The Dominie swerved, but the boat hit something, dully. The children saw it as it came alongside, the body of a man revolving a little, slowly, in the water. The brown, pale face was upturned, the water flowing in thin milky layers over it. The Dominie lunged and caught it by the coat. The boat tipped, and the boys leaned hard to starboard to steady it.

"It's old Nick, all right," said the Dominie, "turning up at last."

He began to unfasten the stringer that was tied to the thwart on which he was sitting, working slowly with one hand, holding the body with the other. The children remembered then what they had heard of old Nick sitting on the railing of the *Elva*, drunk. He had fallen

over backward and had gone down at once. The body
had not risen. It had happened almost a week before
their arrival, when the water in mid-channel must have
been like ice.

The Dominie ran the point of the stringer through the
coat collar, fastened it in a half hitch, and turned the
body over. The coat was unbuttoned, and he buttoned
it. When he had finished, the sleeves of his gray flannel
shirt were wet halfway to the elbow. He passed the end
of the stringer to Scott, who made it fast on his side of
the boat as far astern as he could. Then he turned the
boat and rowed slowly in the direction of the post office.

The boat moved forward with a gliding, jerking
motion. The body, trailing behind to one side, made it
slew around, and every so often Scott said to his father,
"Hard on your right, sir."

The rowlocks creaked, paused, creaked to the Dominie's short, even stroke, and the burden they were towing
raised the water in a ripple that splashed irregularly,
sounding like the ripple caused by a stringerful of fish.
John turned and looked carefully at his brother for a
moment, but Scott was watching the water ahead of
them. The Dominie frowned a little as he rowed, and
once Edith put out her hand and touched the wet gunwale beside her, as if to reassure herself about something.
The wood was cold, and she withdrew her hand quickly
and sat on it, to warm it. Beside her feet were the hap-
hazard coils of the anchor line, and the anchor, gal-
vanized metal splashed with pale mud, the flanges
upturned. A motion of the poncho had spilled a trickle
of water between her bare knees, and she held them
close together.

The river behind them widened almost out of sight. Ahead of them it narrowed, the islands drawing close together for the turn at the Point. They passed a channel stake, a big timber painted black with a number in white, and anchored to the bottom of the river. The weight of moving water tipped it to a forty-five-degree angle with the surface of the river, and as it hung there it revolved, first in one direction and then in the other, but the surface of the river was smooth because the water was very deep.

They went on in toward shore where the current was less strong, and then upstream again to the post office dock. The post office and the postmaster's house stood near the shore. The hill rose abruptly behind the buildings, carrying the dark pines high above. The houses could be entered from the back at the second story by a gallery which ran out level with the hill. A flight of wooden steps came down the hill between the two houses, and from it a boardwalk ran out straight with the line of the dock. A big pile of broken gray rock made a sort of lagoon in front of the dock. It had been dumped there when the channel was being cut and dredged, and no one had ever bothered to take it away. The post office was closed, and the shades were drawn in the house next door. There was no porch to either house, only a straight shingled front with a peaked gable at the top. The wood, that was silvery in dry weather, was black now.

The Dominie hallooed, holding to the edge of the dock with his right hand. A door at the back of the post office opened, and the son of the postmaster came out, bareheaded. He was a big blond fellow. He came down the dock toward them in a half run, lurching with a sort of heavy grace. His feet, in the brown canvas shoes, made little noise, but the planks of the dock sprang slightly under his step. When he saw what they had brought, he drew his breath in between his teeth and lower lip in a whistling sound and swore softly.

He said, "Just moor the old boy to the dock, Perfessor, and I'll take care of him—telephone the Soo and all that. Think I'd better get into my waders before I try to take him ashore, though."

"You can keep the stringer," the Dominie said.

The stone pile hid the dock from sight quickly as they rowed away. The Dominie asked Edith if she was cold, and she said no.

In the cabin they hurried out of their wet clothes and into dry ones. Their shoes were set in a row on the brick hearth to dry, and they all ran around barefoot. The collie puppy got in everyone's way, his cold nose and soft warm fur touching the bare ankles. He was brown with white feet as if he had just stepped out of a pan of milk. The Dominie decided to make pancakes and the children's mother turned the kitchen over to him. She sat by the lamp, rocking and knitting, and the Dominie shouted remarks to her from the kitchen. He was very gay and gentle, looking at the children with a sort of whimsical concern and teasing them.

In the morning the sun was out and the world glistened. Edith ran along the sand in her bathing suit. Her feet did not dent the sand, but where she stepped the pressure of her foot brought a film of water to the surface, which shone and disappeared. The sun was high and hot. The boys were already diving from the end of the government dock. The dock and the red-and-yellow warehouse were reflected upside down, almost inch for inch. Edith stood looking into the clear water, letting the ripples nibble at her toes. The Dominie sauntered along the shore, smoking, and kicking at the pale drift of wet rushes. He said gently, "Afraid of the river this morning?"

"No," she answered, looking up in surprise. "Ought I to be?"

"No," he said. "I think not."

Summer Parties

THEY WENT THERE because they liked to go someplace after supper, and because they liked Merle and because Mrs. Butler never seemed to mind how much noise they made or how they mussed up the house. The Butlers were living that summer in the old red cottage with the outside stairway. There were only the three of them—Mrs. Butler, Merle, and Claudine, who was just nine. Merle was eighteen, a drowsy, good-natured girl with a pretty oval face and drooping shoulders. She never seemed quite awake or quite aware of herself except when she was dancing. Even then she danced in a sort of dream. She had soft brown hair that curled about her cheeks and was pinned up in a loose bun at the back of her neck. She didn't like to fish and not very much to swim. As for hiking, the thought never entered her head. She spent hours in the hammock on the porch, or she helped her mother with the housework. She did anything you asked her to quite willingly, but she almost never thought of anything to do herself. She never got sunburned or tanned, but at the end of the summer the color in her face was a little deeper, a little warmer. She sang all the popular songs, knowing the words about halfway through.

Rummy Blake and the two Atwood boys and Maretta Hotchkiss were the regular gang, and sometimes the young man from the inn whom they called Morpheus.

After supper while Maretta was still doing the dishes Rummy Blake would whistle from the river and come into the house to wait for her, amusing himself by chinning himself on the porch rafters while she washed her hands and smoothed her hair. They'd go in the canoe, not because the Butlers were on the other side of the river, but because it was pleasant to be on the water at that hour.

At the Butlers' there'd be a fire in the living room, and some new dance records. They punched holes in the old records and put them on off center. The phonograph was an old one with a tin horn like a morning glory. They used the loud steel needles and put a pillow in the horn to muffle the noise. Rummy was learning to stand on his head that summer. They danced some, and when the matting made the floor seem too slow they engaged in acrobatics and pillow fights. The Atwood boys were ex-servicemen, one of them with the Croix de Guerre. They were both very handsome and up on all the latest steps. The Croix de Guerre was the better-looking. He was lithe and dark with a little black mustache, and he used to dance cheek to cheek with Merle, who was exactly the right size and complexion for him. They looked charming together. Rummy was huge and bearlike, with large good-looking features still in an unfinished stage, but roughly blocked out; pleased with being so strong and still exploring the possibilities of his strength. His feet, which were so often in the air, were clothed in blunt Canadian shoepacks. His father was rich, having made a fortune in paper tags, and Rummy would inherit the business.

Mrs. Butler was a woman of considerable energy and direction. She went berrying constantly, and put down quantities of wild strawberry and raspberry jam, and her nose was always red and peeling from long hours in the hot berry patches. In the evenings she sat by the fire, leaning her elbow on her knee, her chin in her hand, the blunt strong fingers curving up over her mouth. She gazed into the fire or watched the children, never interfering, but ready to talk if one of them sat down near her. Often she made them hot chocolate or had ice cream for them in the freezer. She was not a pretty woman, but her dark eyes were bright, and she smiled in a generous friendly way, having no secrets.

People occasionally said that she was trying to catch Rummy for Merle, and Maretta Hotchkiss, when she heard this, thought such people vulgar.

Morpheus was loafing on the built-in bench by the fireplace, one foot on the floor and one on the edge of the bench, his knee propping up an illustrated magazine. Maretta borrowed a cigarette from him and sat down beside him. She wore khaki riding breeches and a slip-over sweater. Her collar, which had been freshly starched, was very crumpled, and she was hot and mussed from wrestling with Rummy. She made herself comfortable and lighted the cigarette, and Claudine came across the room and leaned against her knee heavily.

"Leave Maretta alone, babe," said Mrs. Butler.

Claudine sighed and went around beside Morph, put her arm around his neck, and pretended to look at the magazine with him. He took no notice of her save to blow his tobacco smoke in her direction. She fanned it away with her free hand, leaning hard on his shoulder. She looked very much like Merle, except that her hair was a pale brown, almost a gold, and her face browner. It was a smooth oval, the features somewhat larger and fuller than Merle's, but the same features. Her eyes were a cloudy gray, with long honey-colored lashes. She was really very pretty. Her hands were dirty, and she was wearing four or five of the little solder rings that used to come on sticks of candy. The gang had no objection to her, except that she was often sulky and was always grabbing ahold of their hands when they were busy, or wanting to sit on their knees. She was getting too heavy to be such a baby, they thought.

"Leave Morph alone, Claudine," her mother said. "Morph, if she bothers you, shove her away."

"D'you hear that, Claudine?" said Morph casually.

Mrs. Butler moved her chair nearer the bench and said, "Maretta, what would you think of me buying the old Hodges place?"

"What for?" said Maretta.

"So we could have more room for parties—this is an ugly old hole—it'd be nice to ask some of Merle's friends from Detroit to come up for a few weeks during the summer. We could have grand house parties over there."

"It's so far away," objected Maretta.

"Oh, but you've all got boats. I can get it quite cheap. There's the cutest little playhouse in the yard, with a real fireplace."

"That's for me," said Claudine.

"Shut up, Claudine," said Mrs. Butler. "It would make a nice guesthouse."

"It's a lovely place over there," said Maretta. "Wouldn't it take an awful lot of fixing? It's been empty so long."

"Sure it would, but I could do a lot of it myself. What's life for?" said Mrs. Butler.

"What do you think of going across the river to live?" Maretta said to Merle later in the evening, when they were dishing up hot chocolate in the kitchen.

"Oh, I don't care," said Merle. "I like it all right here."

The room had grown hot and full of cigarette smoke. They sat around on the floor, drinking their chocolate cautiously. The phonograph was silenced.

"Well," said Rummy in a little while, "what do you say we wash the dishes and go home?"

"Never mind about the dishes," said Mrs. Butler, "but the evening's yet young."

"I'm sleepy," said Rummy, stretching himself. "Come on, Maretta." Maretta got up obediently.

Outside Rummy linked his arm through hers and flashed the bug light about their feet. It made the grass a sharp unnatural green. A heavy dew had fallen, but the night was clear, and the air fresh after the hot room. They breathed deeply of it. "It's like a drink of water," said Rummy. They went down past the fence to Miss Molly's garden. The faint spicy fragrance of pinks and tangled flower stalks came to them. They looked up at the sky, in which there was no moon but millions of stars whose light fell on their lifted faces like big flakes of snow. Maretta stepped into the water up to her ankle, getting into the canoe. In the darkness the river seemed to be overbrimming its banks.

"You know," said Rummy as the canoe floated forward into the darkness, "Claudine is getting to be an awful brat."

Maretta Hotchkiss rowed slowly down the river. It was a calm morning. The sun burned softly on her hands and bare arms, on the blistered green paint of the gunwale. The bailing can knocked gently back and forth at each pull of the oars. The shouts of someone watering a team at the Canadian shore came to her, pure and small, floated on the water, together with the jingling of the harness and the footfalls of the horses, splashing and stamping.

It was early June, and another summer. Merle was dead. She had died very suddenly in the winter. Mrs. Butler had bought the Hodges place, before Merle's death, and now she had moved into it, with Claudine.

Maretta passed the red house where they had had so many good times last summer. They had all been so foolish—she was a year older. She thought that even if Merle were still alive they couldn't have such good times this year. Rummy was different this year too. His father wasn't well. He had heart trouble, and Rummy was doing more things around the place. She had asked him to come with her this morning, pausing at the Blakes' long dock, holding to the dock with one hand and keeping the boat in position with one oar dipped in the water.

She said, "Come on down and call on Ma Butler."

He said, "I've lots to do. I've been down there once, anyway. No good reason to go again."

As she shoved off and started downstream he called, "I'll be around this afternoon to go swimming."

She nodded, watching him turn and walk back to the boathouse. He was big, and thick around the shoulders. It made him look a little stooped sometimes.

Mrs. Butler was glad to see her. She came out of the house briskly, a hammer in one hand. She wore a mob-cap and a big gingham apron, the apron pocket sagging from a handful of nails. She wiped her face with a corner of the apron and put her arms about Maretta, giving her a brusque, strong hug. They sat down on the railing. There was only one chair on the porch and neither wanted to take it. Sawdust and wood cuttings littered the steps. They had been mending the porch roof, which had collapsed completely at one end under the heavy snow. Old tattered shingles lay below the bridal wreath and rosebushes. There were no curtains in the windows yet.

"I'm keeping busy, Maretta," said Mrs. Butler. "My God, it's the only thing to do. Plenty of work around the old place. Some days I'm glad I got it, and some days I hate the sight of it. You never saw such an old wreck. And pretty nearly everything stolen from the inside of it. I imagine I'd know where to find some of the things, too, if I cared to drive around the island a bit. But I don't care. Let 'em keep 'em."

"It's lovely over here," said Maretta. "Do you like it better than the other side?"

Mrs. Butler paused, turned her head a little, and gave Maretta a shrewd reproachful glance.

"You know well enough, Maretta Hotchkiss, that I'd never've left the other side except for one reason, and that was so Merle and her friends could have better times. My God," she said abruptly, "sometimes I can't believe it yet."

Maretta looked down at the cedar railing and began to pick off minute shreds of bark. There was a short silence, then Mrs. Butler said, almost fretfully, "Why don't the gang come down and see me? Claudine, she hasn't got a soul to play with, poor little thing. She misses you so."

Maretta said, "There's almost nobody here except Rummy and me."

"That's it. It's just Rummy I'm surprised at," said Mrs. Butler. "Down at our house every night last summer, and plenty of ice cream and cake I made for him, too. Now he won't even come near me."

"He's busier this summer," said Maretta. "Mr. Blake isn't very well."

"Oh, he isn't so busy he couldn't come down here once in a while," said Mrs. Butler knowingly. She laughed harshly. "Well, he was here once. Came down to say he was sorry, and all that."

"Don't you believe he's sorry?" asked Maretta.

"Oh yes," said Mrs. Butler, her voice relaxing. "I guess he's sorry. I guess you're all sorry enough. Did you see Claudine yet?"

"No," said Maretta. "Where is she?"

"Around here somewhere. Oh, babe! Oh, Claudine! Come'n say hello to Maretta."

Claudine came slowly out of the house and sat down in the rocker. She said, "Hello, Maretta."

"Been primping, I guess," said her mother. "She don't

make herself very useful, this one. But she's all we've got, and we love her."

She reached out a strong red hand and patted Claudine on the shoulder. Claudine made no gesture. She looked at Maretta with a slow languid stare, her gray eyes veiled, her figure drooping against the back of the chair. She had on a pink cotton dress and dirty white socks. Her knees were brown and bare. Maretta thought, "There's something insulting about the kid." She liked Mrs. Butler, but she wanted to leave.

Mrs. Butler followed her down to the gate.

"Come again. Come often, Maretta. And you can tell Rummy Blake from me he's a cupboard guest. Yes sir, that's what he is—a cupboard guest." Her voice hardened again.

Maretta crossed the road where a few sheep were lying in the cedar shade. In her embarrassment she had nothing to say. She turned and waved and hurried along the grassy shore to the rowboat. The sun was almost at noon.

Nell

〰〰〰〰〰〰〰〰〰〰〰〰〰〰〰〰〰〰〰〰〰〰〰〰〰〰〰〰〰

THE ROAD on which Cora was walking followed the river, running along on a high green bank. Below there was a sandy beach and a long stretch of shallow water reaching almost to the edge of the channel. The river had built a wide submerged sand bar, here where it turned. On each side of the road the grass was cropped close, fitting each rise and hollow of the ground as the skin of a peach the fruit. Here and there were clumps of blue iris mixed with buttercups. On the right the ground sloped gently away toward farms and woods.

The day was sunny, the water very blue. The balsams and cedars which crowded to the edge of the opposite shore stood tiny and clear. Small figures in blue or white were moving about on the narrow beaches and the docks. She caught a flash of light from the wet side of a boat.

The Catholic church was ahead of her, behind the shadow of its trees. By the wooden gate in the cool shadow she paused. About her feet the earth was brown, littered with twigs and mast. In front of the church, in the yard, the weeds had grown very high. The long grass had drooped and fallen over the path like waves of soft hair. She wondered if the door was locked. Once or twice during the summer she had heard a bell sounding over the still water in the early morning, but service was conducted very seldom. She had never yet been inside the building.

She hesitated, her hand on the gate, then lifted the rusty latch and entered the yard. A few leaves lay on the church steps. The doors were painted brown, with panels of white, from which the paint was flaking lightly. She opened the door and stepped directly into the one room of the church.

It was white and silent. Long bars of sunlight fell through the three high windows and were reflected gently from the walls. The floor was bare. At the far end upon the altar table someone had arranged fresh flowers in vases of green and white pressed glass—daisies and sweet william, but mostly daisies.

The quiet of the room shut her away from the summer noises outside, the slight sound of the water, the wind in the trees, the barking of the heavily furred collies at the farm gates. She sat down in one of the bare straight pews and folded her hands in her lap. She was a small woman. Her head was large, with a wide brow, her hair gray and pinned in flat coils close to her head. At the back of her neck it was still brown, and the loose ends curled. She wore a man's gray sweater.

She began to think of an old woman with a white, heavy face and coarse, unhealthy skin, a hard mouth with full sensuous lips, lips pale and wet, a face fretful and complaining, broken suddenly by bursts of rowdy humor. The old woman leaned over a banister, shouting

to someone in the hall below. Her disordered white hair
fell in locks about her face. She held a dirty silk kimono
gathered about her great shaking body. It was Nell, her
half sister. The children had written:

"We give Mother all the dope she wants now. It keeps
her happy and eases the pain."

"I like it, Cory," Nell had said once, her brown eyes
bright with mockery. "It gives me a good time."

With the image of Nell the image of the house on
Sheldon Avenue came into her mind. It had not been
uncomfortable, after all. Neither had it been very attractive. It was larger than they needed, but that had
made it possible for Cora to ask her mother and Nell to
come to them for a visit. She gave them the large downstairs sitting room, making it into a bedroom. It had a
good south light, and she put some ferns in the window
to make it gay.

She remembered Nell standing before the walnut
étagère with its little mirrors, knobs, and gilded tassels.
She was powdering her cheeks with pink, and when she
had finished she rubbed a pink paste on her lips.

"I wish you wouldn't paint yourself," said Cora. "At
your age it doesn't look right. Makes you look bawdy."

"Ah bah bawdy," said Nell with good humor. "I don't
care."

She put on her hat and knotted a scarf of pink chiffon
about her throat.

"Where are you going?" asked Cora.

"Anywhere. Must get out of here. The whole house
smells of babies' didies and cabbage soup. And Mother
sits by the window all day and hems dustcloths. My
Gawd. I want to go and listen to the elevated trains."

"You'd better go back to New York if you feel that way about it," said Cora stiffly.

"Don't get huffy, honey," said Nell. "You know I like to be with you, and the children need a rest from me. I only get so tired of all this suburban peace."

Their mother sat beside the ferns at the window and rocked. A patch of sunlight moved up and down over her knee with regular motion. She offered nothing to the conversation. Nell collected her gloves and her coin purse, and kissed her mother. At the door she kissed Cora and patted her affectionately. Cora said without rancor, "Well, have a good time."

Nell had been the child of her mother's first marriage. She was much older than Cora, and her children were grown when Cora's family was just beginning. They were a helter-skelter lot. Their grandmother found them a little wearing. She liked better to be with Cora and Cora's quiet little boy. She liked the new baby and the tranquil, busy monotony of the days. She did not mind the smell of cabbage soup.

Cora laid a place for Nell but did not wait supper for her. She was used to her sister's casual attitude regarding the hours of meals. But as they sat about the table, eating, and talking a little, she grew more and more troubled by the suppressed anxiety in her mother's face.

The little boy went to bed. Cora's husband locked himself up with his books. The two women washed the dishes and dried them. Cora saw her mother's mouth growing grim and tight.

"Don't worry, Mother," she said. "Nell's a grown woman. She can take care of herself."

"Maybe," her mother answered.

About nine o'clock she came to where Cora was sitting and said, "I'm going to bed. Don't wait up for her, Cory."

Cora followed her mother into her room and sat on the edge of the bed, watching the old woman undress. The old body was like her own. She saw it as a young body, clouded with age. She saw, with every deliberate gesture, the intention to ignore anxiety emphasizing what it was intended to hide. She tucked the covers about the shoulders of the grim little old woman, opened the windows, and turned out the gas jet.

She had the house to herself then, but did not want to read or go to bed. At last she put on her hat and coat and went outdoors.

The night was warm for fall, and rather muggy. She walked north, toward Lake Street, between the wide lawns and the darkened houses. Elm trees were planted in the parkway at regular distances, and their trunks cast oblique shadows on the sidewalk, pointing in the direction in which she was going. In the middle of the block a tree cast two shadows, dimly, pointing in opposite directions. Then the arc light at the next corner took up the work of illuminating the grass, and the shadows fell across the sidewalk toward her feet.

At the elevated tracks, so called, she turned and walked along with them. The tracks ran on the ground here, behind a long fence. The wheels spat and shrieked on the steel rails. She paused in front of a movie theater. It was the end of a show, and the audiences were changing. The lights were bright over the heads of the shifting, talking people, the little white ticket booth, the gaudy billboards. A popcorn man stood at the sidewalk's edge

with his lighted wagon. She looked through the crowd
for Nell but did not see her.

At every druggist's window she stopped and peered
past the luminous red and blue or red and green tall
bottles. She came to the corner where the streetcar tracks
crossed those of the elevated. There was a drugstore on
one side of the street and a saloon on the other. On the
far side of the elevated tracks was the embankment for
the Northwestern Railroad. It was cut into by a square
tunnel, dimly lighted, where the rattle of wagons and
the noise of horses' hoofs were jumbled and re-echoed. It
was a dreary corner, and yet there seemed to be a good
deal of life. Four or five men, waiting for the streetcar,
stood in a group at the edge of the sidewalk. A woman
much younger than Nell brushed past her. She wore no
hat, and her skirt dragged in the dirt. She was drunk,
and when she tried to step down into the street she
stumbled. One of the men caught her hand and said,
"Whoopsy daisy, there, old girl." She tried to slap his
face, but he ducked. She stood there with them, waiting
for the car, and the man went on kidding her, spitting
on the ground at her feet.

It was a trivial incident, but it made Cora feel sick,
and she walked home through a slow drizzle that was
just beginning. She went to bed, leaving the light burning, and tried to read. She fell asleep, but could not have
slept for very long, for it was only eleven when she woke.
It was raining hard, then. She went out on the porch for
a last look around. Someone was sitting on the bottom
step. There was enough light from the arc at the corner
to tell that it was Nell.

They got her to bed and called the doctor. Nell, sitting

up in bed, drinking hot water with peppermint in it, insisted that she hadn't had any dope.

"Just one glass of whisky, Cory," she said.

She couldn't remember where she had been or what she had done after that one drink, but her face was sodden like the muddy shoes and wet coat that Cora took into the next room to dry.

That was so long ago.

It had all begun with an illness that had been very long and very painful: cancer. They had checked the advance of the disease for a time. Of late years it had come on again. The doctors had thought it necessary to give her morphine. When the pain began to lessen she found it hard to give up the drug. It worried her, and she tried to substitute whisky. In the end she had succumbed to both, and the death of her husband had made things worse.

Sadness rose in the heart of the small woman in the gray sweater as the shadows were rising slowly among the straight pews and empty corners of the church. She continued to stare at the altar with its country flowers, seeing beyond them Nell as a young lady when she herself was a little girl. Ten years lay between them. Then Cora wore dresses of a blue wool stuff with full skirts and rows of black velvet ribbon stitched on around the hem. Her hair was cropped close to her head. Nell liked to run her hand over the stubby thick curls, and called her sister "Pony."

Nell was slender in those days, with a warm, pale, dusky skin, and lips that glowed. She was very stylish, with a daring that made even the prim dresses of the period attractive and careless like herself. She was lavish with a perfume she had discovered, a musky, spicy odor that Cora loved. Their mother disapproved of it but did not forbid it, and Cora was glad. She liked to finger the square glass bottles that Nell kept on her bureau. They fitted into a square ebony box, four of them. The box was lined with a deep rose brocade.

Nell had many suitors. She received them in the stately formal parlor with its red velvet furniture and heavy carvings in walnut, rosewood, and mahogany. She let Cora hide in the corner behind the big sofa to listen to the conversation. She liked to lead the boys on until they said ridiculous romantic things, but there was almost no hugging or kissing. She was impatient of being touched. She said, "You know, Pony, I'm not much on this Nearer-my-God-to-Thee stuff."

Then one day she ran away to New York with a man from out of town. Her mother and stepfather were very stern about it. Cora was afraid to question them, and for three or four weeks she never heard a word of Nell. Once Cora saw a strange, heavily veiled woman standing in their hall, but she was sent upstairs before she heard her speak. As she turned, however, slowly at the landing, her hand on the smooth cold banister, she caught a whiff of Nell's musky perfume, and when she reached her own room, hers and Nell's, she sat down on the floor and twisted her fingers tightly in great unhappiness, wondering what her mother was saying to Nell in the big gloomy parlor.

Nell wanted to come home. She was tired of her adventure. Her mother said that she might come if she would leave behind her everything, big or little, which that man had bought for her or given to her. Nell ob-

jected. Her mother was firm, and Nell went back to New
York. Long after, Cora tried to think just what it had
cost her mother to watch Nell go down the flagged walk
between the clipped rosebushes, and not call.

Nell came home after two more weeks. She and Cora
were in the upstairs room together. Nell gave her a
brooch, two golden leaves curved about a row of cherries.
No, not cherries. The fine glitter of the gold spikes that
held them, and the faceting, breaking them into petals
of light, made them more like flowers.

"Don't show it to Mother," Nell said, "or I shall have
to go away again. It's the only thing I kept. I had a good
time, and I wanted to bring you a present. It's not very
valuable—they're only garnets."

That same afternoon she said, "I never let him touch
me, Pony. I couldn't stand him when he got too near to
me. But he was good-looking and he took me to the
theater, lots." She laughed. "I don't know what Father
and Mother believe—I don't suppose they believe that,
but it's true."

Pony was wonderfully glad to have her home again.
The next Sunday Nell walked down the aisle of the First
Baptist Church on her stepfather's arm, looking as lovely
as ever. Pony walked behind them, holding her mother's
hand. She thought they were all happy again.

The shadows in the corners of the church were deep,
like dust. The sunlight lay higher and higher in the air.
The place was innocent and calm. Cora sighed and
stirred on the hard bench. This long meditation was all
that she could do for Nell, her dear Nell. She could not
cry. She could not even be sorry. It was too late. It was
time to go home and cook supper for the children, and
tell her husband that Nell was dead.

The House

~~~~~~

THE HOUSE AND BARN were painted yellow with white trim. The house was large, three stories high, with a many-gabled roof. On each ridgepole stood a white wood fence in arabesques. A large covered porch ran from the front of the house halfway around the south side, a white porte-cochere opened on the north to the graveled drive, and there were various small balconies and bay windows which enlarged the simple shape of the building. The barn was big enough for a carriage room, stalls, a manger, and an apartment for the gardener and his family. The barn and the house were surrounded by low bushes, snowball, syringa, yellow spicebush. At the end of the smooth lawn was a small maple grove. Near the barn were the rose garden and the strawberry beds. To the north of the house two or three clumps of purple lilac had made themselves into a small forest. The trees about the house were elm, box elder, pine. When the house was first built, the lawn smoothed, the rose garden planted, the two empty blocks across the street had been cornfields, and the blocks to the north

nothing but prairie, where violets and wild strawberries
grew in the long grass. Little by little, as the suburb
became popular, the vacant lots filled with homes, and
the Wilkey estate was left rather like some old English
hunting ground in the middle of a city. The children
in the neighborhood thought of it as such. It provided
vistas, ambushes, and retreats. No one ever told them
not to climb in the maple trees or chased them off the
roof of the barn. At the end of the block was a pasture
where the old cow grazed. It was surrounded by a board
fence, and a cluster of mulberry trees grew near the
fence. The trees were too frail to climb, and Frances
Donalson and the redheaded Niles boy used to sit on
top of the fence, picking berries from the lacy boughs
and watching the cow wade through deep clover stems.
Frances Donalson's grandmother lived in the yellow
house. Her father was Jesse Donalson, a gentle-faced
young man with graying hair and skin. He taught chem-
istry in the high school, and a slight acid odor from the
laboratory clung always to his clothing. Her mother was
Mary Wilkey. Her aunt Roberta and her aunt Kate lived
in the big house with her grandmother, along with her
uncle Archibald and her cousins and second cousins, the
children and grandchildren of Aunt Kate and Uncle
Archie. The second cousins were near her own age,
slightly older, however, and more advanced in their
amusements. They didn't think much of sliding down
the barn roof. The first cousins were old enough to be
her aunts. There were five of them. Three of them
were married and had homes of their own, but since
they were always dropping in for supper, for lunch, to
use the sewing machine, to visit Grandma, to visit each

other, to plan parties and expeditions, they might as well
have lived there, as far as it concerned the imagination
of the little cousin or the labors of Annie.

Annie lived on the top floor. The top floor was attic
except for Annie's room, which was plastered and ceiled.
Frances sometimes went upstairs to visit her, shutting
the stairway door behind her carefully and climbing the
steep dark way toward the dusty sunlight. The attic
smelled of warm wood, mice, and old boxes. It was like a
front yard to Annie's room, which smelled of soap and
prayer books.

In her aunt Roberta's room, which was on the first
floor, were a porcelain mandarin who nodded his head, a
rose jar smelling of cinnamon, and a snowstorm in a
globe. When you held the glass ball still in your hand
the snow settled gently upon the roof of the tiny mill
and on the small green bushes. When you shook it the
snow rose again into the air and it stormed. Under the
bed were many boxes full of carefully tied packages. A
few of these were letters, but most of them were old
theater programs, church programs, rolls of wrapping
paper, brown paper bags, smoothed and folded carefully.
There were a great many of the little gay paper fans, ad-
vertising summer drinks, which the drugstores give away
in hot weather. Aunt Roberta saved things without
knowing why she was saving them. No one was allowed
to touch them. When she went out walking she carried
her pocketbook, an extra wrap, and a brown paper parcel.
Sometimes she had forgotten what was in the parcel, but
she carried it because she would not have felt properly
equipped without it. Once she had suffered from a disease of the skin, and her legs had been heavily bandaged.

Over the bandages she wore a pair of white stockings, and over the white stockings a dark pair. After her skin was healed she was persuaded to give up the bandages, but she never gave up the white stockings. Frances was very fond of her aunt Roberta. They went walking together, and Roberta bought paper dolls, whole regiments by the sheet, and sticks of sweet paraffin gum, done up in colored wrappers with fringed ends. Sitting on the hassock by her aunt Roberta's armchair, Frances cut out the regiments and arranged them in military fashion on the floor, and her aunt leaned over her, watching in admiration.

Roberta was the oldest of Mrs. Wilkey's daughters. Her hair, once brown, had turned an even iron gray, become wiry and crisp. It looked frowzy, no matter how often it was combed. Her skin was brown, and her eyes shortsighted. She refused to wear glasses, and scowled, even when she smiled. One day Mary, entering by the front door, had found Frances and Roberta in the hall, weeping and clinging to each other. As far as she could find out from their answers, Kate had scolded Roberta for making Frances cry, Roberta had cried, and Frances had wept for Roberta. They were joined together against Kate, the old child and the young child comforting each other.

James Wilkey left no large oil portrait of himself to gaze down upon his grandchildren from the parlor wall. There were a few daguerreotypes in velvet cases in Mrs. Wilkey's top bureau drawer, but the house itself was a more accurate portrait. The height of the doors, the largeness and uprightness of the furniture, the spaciousness of the rooms, seemed to indicate an erect, gray-

coated figure moving among them. Mrs. Wilkey's plump
short person passing with rapid step from dining room
to living room, from living room to hall, oversaw these
rooms for someone else. As she grew older she went
about the house less and sat more in her large sunny
bedroom on the second floor. Kate also kept to her own
room a great deal, being a semi-invalid, a heavy, white-
haired woman, lying in bed with a faded pink bed jacket
about her shoulders. Kate's children filled the house.

They were a gay lot. They never had enough money
to dress as they would have liked to, but what money
they had they spent on clothes, and were endlessly revis-
ing old clothes, to be a little more smart, a little more
fresh. They left their scissors and tape measures on the
parlor chairs, along with scraps of ribbons, basting
threads, faded bunches of cloth flowers. They made their
own hats, beginning sometimes fifteen minutes before
the hour when they wanted to wear them. They had
many beaux, but when beaux were short they com-
mandeered their father, calling him Archie and tweak-
ing his necktie. They would take off his gray felt hat
and put it back on his head at a rakish angle, and kiss
him behind the ears. They liked classy shows, but liked
cheap shows better than no shows at all, and on a sultry
summer afternoon they would take Archie by the arm
and march him off to Forest Park, to the roller coasters
and scenic railways. They would ride out in an open car,
watching the dust and the torn papers fly up from the
street at the rush of the wheels, and after the fun in the
park was over they would cross the street to a cheap Ger-
man restaurant, and have beer and cheese sandwiches
with rye bread.

Archibald Martin had a way of getting jobs easily, but he had a way of losing them too. When he was working he contributed his share to the expenses of the house, and when he was out of work he didn't. When he was out of work he spent most of his time at home, which pleased the girls and made things merrier. They said, "After all, Gran's rich." He made a few investments. Some of them were successful, but several times he was obliged to apply to his mother-in-law for help, when luck had been against him. Then he had a famous chance to make good money and pay back all he owed, if Gran would only lend him a little capital to start things off.

The old lady objected. Martin sat with hurt, surprised eyes, his fingers fidgeting with the ends of his sandy beard. He said, "You have always been so generous. I thought I could surely count on you, and it's all for your good. In fact it's mainly for the sake of paying back what I owe you. I don't like to owe you money."

Mrs. Wilkey said dryly, "I don't object to your owing me money, Archibald, or to giving it to you either. In a way, all that I have given you has been yours, or would have been yours sooner or later. It's simply that, if this goes on, there will presently be nothing at all to give you. I don't know that it's exactly fair to your daughters, either. You're spending their inheritance."

"But, Gran," he said, "I am going to restore their inheritance."

Mrs. Wilkey deliberately clipped the end of a thread from a sock she was mending. "Very well," she said at length. "If the girls consent to your investing this money, I will let you have it, but I want it plainly understood that you are, all of you, receiving your share of the inheritance now."

She began to hunt for a fresh needle in the red cotton tomato, and as she said nothing more, and did not look up from her search, Martin rose and went awkwardly and silently out of the room.

The girls were delighted at the prospect of rehabilitating the family fortunes, and Gran drew the check that Archibald required.

He bought a bunch of sweet peas for Gran on his way home from the city that night, and Gran was pleased with them. He bought them at the secondhand flower stand on the lower bridge of the elevated station, and they withered quickly, but that did not matter.

When Sue, Kate's oldest daughter, divorced her husband, there had been nothing else to do but come home to the yellow house, bringing the two children, Leo and Sophia. Sue got herself a job in a firm of interior decorators and paid her share of the expenses of the house. Gran gave her the barn for an office and workshop, and she set up business for herself, moving her worktables into the carriage room and wheeling the antique surrey and barouche into the corner. It was too late to sell them. Nobody wanted a barouche. Nobody wanted a low green cutter with pictures painted on its sides. Will, the divorced husband, came regularly to see her, preferring to bring the monthly check in person. "Alimony night," Sue would call, running upstairs. "I must get into my chauncy earrings." Will had been divorced for drinking, and he lived in hopes of conquering himself and being reinstated in his family, but Sue liked him better as a lover than as a husband. He was a slender dark-eyed man with a silky black mustache. He drew marvelous pictures for the children and always had a pocketful of finely pointed pencils.

"Come now," Mary heard Sophia saying to Frances, "my father's here, and your father's coming over, and you're going to stay for supper. Come and tell Annie and hear her say, 'With the help of God and a couple of policemen.'" Mary stood in the hall, holding the telephone, waiting for her husband to answer. Presently she heard the children in the kitchen.

"Can you get supper for four extra tonight?" said Sophia, and Annie answered, "With the help of God and a couple of policemen I can. Get out of here now, the two of you."

The children tiptoed past her, very pleased, and went into the parlor to beg for pictures.

It was the middle of February, a week before Gran's eightieth birthday. The house was sheeted in a sticky, sleety rain, and the afternoon was dark. In Sue's room Sophia, Frances, and Roberta were making paper roses by gaslight. Sue looked in occasionally to see how things were going and issue directions. Marianne Martin came in once or twice but did not stay. She was spending the afternoon with Mrs. Wilkey to keep the old lady busy.

Frances and Sophia were curling the edges of petals on a hatpin. They stretched the centers a little with their thumbs, making them hollowed and flowerlike, and dropped them into a box. Sometimes Frances shook the box and raked the pink shells about lightly with the tips of her fingers, thinking of her aunt Roberta's rose jar. She liked the paper petals as well as the real ones. By

and by Cousin Sue and Cousin Marianne would build
them up into flowers, fastening them to a stem, binding
the stem with green and attaching green leaves. There
were already big boxes of flowers in the closet and under
the bed. Her aunt Roberta was cutting out petals from a
pattern, breathing heavily as she worked and stopping
often to watch the little girls. The house was full of con-
spiracy. When it came time for Frances to go home to
supper, Cousin Sue brushed her off with a whisk broom.

"It would never do to have you running in to kiss
Gran all covered with pink scraps. She'd smell a mouse.
Yes ma'am, smell a mouse and see it brewing in the air."

When the birthday came a long table made of boards
and sawhorses was set up in the big red-curtained dining
room, and decorated with pink and green. The room was
festooned with roses and lighted with candles, and there
were pink and green baskets full of nuts at everyone's
place. There was a big white mint candy, the size of a
cooky, for everyone, too, marked in pink sugar with
"Eighty." The birthday cake was in the kitchen, waiting
to be lighted, but Frances and Sophia had seen it before
Annie chased them out. It had eighty little pink candles
around it in a ring.

The children and grandchildren and great-grand-
children, and the sons- and grandsons-in-law gathered in
Mrs. Wilkey's room, upstairs, and descended to the
dining room in a grand march. Mrs. Wilkey headed the
procession on the arm of Archibald Martin, and Frances
and Roberta brought up the rear, quivering with excitement. Annie stood at the door in a fresh white apron to
usher them in.

There were eighteen of them at the table. They jostled each other and talked all at once, resembling each other, if taken in the proper order, like the progressive chords in a harmony which lead from one key to another.

Annie brought in the cake with its circle of little flames, and Marianne pounded on the table and cried, "Speech, Grandma, speech." Mrs. Wilkey stood up, the candles making funny upward shadows on her face, and everyone cheered. Sue said, "Don't cry, Gran." Mrs. Wilkey looked down the long table. The tears shone on her cheeks, she made her speech, and cut the cake. Frances did not eat her white candy with the pink letters, but saved it to look at.

One morning in the autumn after Gran's eightieth birthday Mary sat with her mother in the upstairs room. The elms were turning brown. The trolley cars on Lake Street, a block away, sounded muffled and far, as if the haze in the air had enveloped sound as well as form. Both women were sewing. Mrs. Wilkey seemed to put off what she had to say as long as she could. When she had folded her work and laid it aside she made her announcement in a voice from which old age had gradually withdrawn the timbre.

"I've sold the house, Mary."

"Oh, Mother."

"I haven't yet told Kate. The agreement allows me the use of it as long as I shall live, and the money is to be paid to the estate after my death. The Martin tribe will have to shift for itself. I am very sorry, but it had to be done." She looked about the room with affection and some regret, and said humorously, "I don't intend to die for some time.

"For Roberta I have set aside twenty thousand. I should like to leave you as much. If, after Roberta's twenty thousand and twenty for you, there is anything left, it goes to the Martins. That's all in my will. But I will not saddle you with Roberta. You will be her guardian, but she will not have to live with you. She will be happier if she doesn't, and it will be more fair to you and Jesse."

Mary moved her lips to form a protest but did not speak it.

"The Martins have already had their share. I have been very weak with 'em. I love them too much, but while my head's clear I'm arranging not to be weak with 'em after my death."

She finished up the conversation in much the same manner in which she finished and folded up her work, and Mary was not invited to discuss the subject with her.

Early that winter Mrs. Wilkey died. Kate and Mary were alone in the house with her. Kate was dazed and made stupid by the event. She sat in an armchair in her mother's room, staring at the floor or the foot of the bed, her face dull with unrealized sorrow. Mary had to meet the girls and Roberta and tell them of the death of someone who belonged almost more to them than to herself. At least, it seemed so at that moment.

On the morning of the funeral she stood at the house door, leaning her head against the cold wood of the jamb. Flowers, tied with a purple ribbon, hung there above the bell, close to her face. They had a coolness which seemed apart from the coolness of the morning, either less or

more cool, Mary could not think. It was snowing a little
from a clouded sky, the flakes falling upon the crust of
snow already fallen, and masking the brown of the sidewalk that had been cleaned. A few flakes rose now and
then from the ground, joining the hesitant turmoil in
the air, and falling again. Mrs. Wilkey lay in the parlor,
surrounded by flowers. Sue and Marianne had filled the
coffin with pink roses. Now that she lay still, the small
hands, the large head and strong throat, all the compact
old body assumed a great dignity. Roberta had spent the
morning near her, refusing to leave the room. When the
guests began to arrive Mary went into the parlor and put
her arm about Roberta, who wept again, at the touch of
affection. Then they went upstairs hand in hand, exiled
from the dead.

When the will was read, some days later, and the
estate gone over, there was found to be the twenty thousand for Roberta and eighteen thousand for Mary. The
expenses of the funeral had to be charged to the estate,
as well as all the flowers the Martins had ordered, for
they themselves had no money.

They said to Jesse Donalson, "We wanted Gran to
have a real funeral, and we thought that part of the
estate, at least, was ours."

Mary had not been present at the reading of the will.
The doctor had ordered her to stay in bed and rest for a
month. Marianne came to see her, sitting in a chair at
the foot of the bed, looking across the stretch of white
counterpane at Mary's wan face. Marianne was very
pretty and the emotion of the ten days had made her
features more mobile and alive. She drew the fingers of
her glove slowly through her closed hand, hesitating.

"Aunt Mary," she said, "I'm sorry you're sick, but I came to talk about the will. It doesn't seem to be the way Gran meant it to be, and we feel—all of us—that Gran would be disappointed that we weren't remembered. Bitterly disappointed. Gran said that she meant each of us to have two thousand dollars—that is, outside of what Father and Mother were to have." She stopped. Her lip quivered a little. "I don't really mind for myself so much. I don't need it—much—but it is hard on Eleanor and Katrina. Sue has her business, and Debby has Tim, who is well enough off."

She stopped again, and Mary looked at the ceiling, which seemed sallow and grimy. Her body felt cold under the warmth of the blanket. She said, "I guess Jesse and I can spare you something—something for you and Eleanor and Katrina, your two thousand each, if Gran wanted that."

Marianne stood up, looking curiously regretful. She said, "Well, good-bye, Aunt Mary. You always were a dear." She went toward the door. As she went out she turned and blew a kiss from the palm of her hand.

Mary did not see her again. Marianne and her husband went West to live. Eleanor went to New York, to go on the stage, if she could. Katrina went with her. Mary never heard if they managed it or not. Even Sue moved to New York finally, and none of them wrote to Mary. They were none of them any good at letters.

Little Hellcat

$\sim\sim\sim\sim\sim\sim\sim\sim\sim\sim\sim\sim\sim\sim\sim\sim\sim\sim\sim\sim$

D R. SCHMIDT'S MINE. He's short but
he's nice. He's so short that I thought for a while I
wouldn't ever be engaged to him. And I used to be afraid
of doctors. You wouldn't believe it.

"After we're married of course I won't live at the hospital, but I'll go on being a nurse. I'm going around with
him to help catch babies."

"Catch babies?"

"As they come out. He's so nice. And he's got almost
the bluest eyes I ever saw. I think it's nice to have blue
eyes in a man, don't you? Because it's about the only
way they can afford to be pretty, haven't you noticed?"

"You've got pretty eyes yourself."

"My eyes are gray. My eyes are gray, and I've got black
hair and this kind of a skin because my grandma on my
mother's side was Irish."

She took off her cap and ran her fingers through her
hair until it stood out around her head. Then she
smoothed it down neatly, and smiled, and put on her cap.

"The bluest eyes I ever saw belonged to Mr. Hansen.

No, he wasn't a doctor. He was a friend of Dr. Schmidt's, and he lived over at Kettlestone. But he used to come over here a lot for dances. He looked like Prince William of Sweden. Did you ever see a picture of Prince William of Sweden? Well, that's the way Mr. Hansen looked, though of course Prince William is more refined-looking. But Mr. Hansen was awfully nice. We used to have fun —Dr. Schmidt and Mr. Hansen and me, and Jorgy. Jorgy used to be supervisor of the floor—Miss Christine Jorgenson—and she and Mr. Hansen were engaged. We used to go to dances lots. Jorgy was a Swede too, and she was all right. She was really pretty nice, mostly. She liked me because I was in love too, and she could confide in me about Mr. Hansen. She was always confiding in me. But Mr. Hansen liked me too—not especially, you know—but just enough to make it nice when we all went out together. So sometimes Jorgy was sore at me because she was a jealous crab, sometimes. She was good-looking but she was too tall. I wouldn't like to be any taller than I am. If I were I couldn't possibly marry Dr. Schmidt."

She sat smiling down at her hands. Then she said seriously, "Something awful happened to me a while ago. I might tell you. I don't think I'd like to tell anyone else.

"You see, Dr. Schmidt and Mr. Hansen had it all fixed up to take us girls to a dance. It was Saturday night, just about a couple of months ago, early in October, and there was a big dance at the Gaiety, and I was sure I had a P.M. coming to me. What's that? Afternoon off. Afternoon and evening right through until seven o'clock the next morning. So the two of them, they talked to me about it, and when we sprang it on Jorgy, why, the superintendent had told her she'd have to stay on that night.

So Mr. Hansen and Doctor said that that was too bad, and we'd all go out together the next time she could get off, and for this night we three 'ud go to the dance just the same, and Mr. Hansen would stag it. So when I told that to Jorgy she said she was very sorry but she'd need me on the floor that night, and I'd have to take my P.M. sometime the next week.

"Well, I was a little sore, because I didn't think she needed me really, and I don't yet. Honestly I don't. But I hunted up Dr. Schmidt and told him; and he said all right; he and Mr. Hansen would go duck shooting up to Little Berry Lake, and if I could get off Sunday afternoon we'd play around a little then. So I said all right, and I told Jorgy and she said all right.

"My, she kept herself awful busy that night trying to keep me busy enough so that I wouldn't think she was just keeping me on because she was jealous. And I didn't let on what I thought, because in a way I was fond of Jorgy.

"There was a funny story happened that night. They brought a little boy in from the coal camp. He was pretty sick. And he was lying there pretty flat with just his nose sticking out, and he was being as good as he could. For such a tough little kid. Then Dr. Howard came in to look him over, and he stopped by the side of the bed and said, 'Well, kid, what's the matter with you?' And the kid said, 'Please, sir, I've got ladies' disease.' And Dr. Howard just roared. 'That's a new name for it,' he said."

"What did he mean?"

"G.C. You're not shocked? That's good.

"Well, and so. Eventually, as they say in the storybooks, I got off duty and went to bed.

"Of course I'm used to getting up early, but you know if you're waked up just a half hour earlier, maybe, than you're used to getting up, it's like being waked up in the middle of the night. It was like that this time. I guess it was really only five-thirty, or maybe it was six, but it was dark, and somebody said there was a long-distance telephone call for me.

"And I got up, and put on my kimono, and went walking down those long corridors over at the dormitory, and downstairs; and I was shivering; and nobody was up yet; and it was like a dream. That was just what it was like.

"And it was Dr. Schmidt. And the first thing he said was, 'I'm all right, sweetheart.'

"So then I knew something was wrong, and I began to shake for honest and truly, and I held on tight to that phone.

"You see, they'd gotten up about four and gone out on the lake in a canoe. And the canoe tipped over and Mr. Hansen was drowned. Dr. Schmidt thought maybe it was because he had on one of those awfully heavy canvas jackets. Anyway, he was drowned, and Dr. Schmidt just held on to the canoe until somebody came after him.

"The sun never did come up that day. It didn't shine once, and it was cold." She paused.

"That *was* awful," agreed the listener.

"No, that wasn't it," said the little nurse. "This was what was awful.

"You see, I got dressed then, because it was almost time to get up anyway. I had part of a cup of coffee, and I got over on the floor, and I met Jorgy.

" 'Did you hear what happened this morning?' she said, real short and sharp.

"And I said yes, and I was trying to think what to say next when she snapped, 'Well, you don't look it!'

"Then I didn't know what to say, and Jorgy said, 'It ain't fair. It ain't fair for you to have all the luck. It ain't fair for me to lose my man and you not to lose yours. I wish it was your man that got drowned. Then maybe you wouldn't look so peaches-and-cream this morning. I wish they'd both got drowned.'

"Then I got mad. I never was so mad before. And I said, 'It's all your fault, Christine Jorgenson, you jealous crab. It's all your fault. 'Cause if you'd let me go to the dance Hansen and Dr. Schmidt wouldn't have gone hunting, and Hansen wouldn't be drowned. It's all your fault!'

"And she began to yell at me out there in the corridor with all the patients listening, and I began to yell at her. I called her a jealous crab, and a damned fool, and she called me a hellcat. A little hellcat."

Sunday Dinner

M R. AND MRS. GUIDICATTI drove in at
the gate, past the house, into the back yard. They stopped
the car and got out. The house was on one side of them,
small, unpainted, a reddish brown from the weathering
of the wood, and the barn at the other, a high, unfinished
structure. A big black-and-white dog, furry, his hair all
over his eyes, got up slowly from the hard hot ground
and wagged his tail dubiously. The back door opened,
and Mrs. Perrault stepped out on the porch.

"Hello there," she said. "You're right on time and
everything."

"Had a fine ride down," said Mr. Guidicatti. "Where's
the old man?"

"Out among the rabbits," said Mrs. Perrault.

"I'll go fetch him in," said Mr. Guidicatti. He crossed
the trampled ground, avoiding stepping on a brood of
little yellow ducks, and disappeared behind the barn.

His wife went up the short steep flight of the back
steps, her coat over one arm, her pocketbook in one hand,
and a crushed brown paper parcel in the other, and was

embraced by Mrs. Perrault. The women went into the house. In the back entry was an electric washing machine and a stack of mops and brooms. They went into the living room, passing through the kitchen. The kitchen took up half of the back of the house, the living room half of the front. There was a table in the middle of the room, and a sideboard in one corner. On the table were schoolbooks, papers, chewed stubs of pencils, a few marbles, a vase of zinnias, a little boy's jacket. On the sideboard were four rows of silver trophy cups, all sizes and shapes. There were two cot beds, some chairs, and an upright piano. There were potted plants on the floor and on the window sills. It was a small room.

Mrs. Guidicatti dropped her coat, pocketbook, and parcel on one of the cots and sat down on the other. She took a deep breath, stretching herself a little, and patted her hair. She was a fine-looking woman of about thirty-five, with an alert strong face and a sort of potential emotionalism. Her hair was short. She wore it parted in the middle and brushed back smoothly behind her ears. She had a high forehead and her hair was very black. A small short-coated white dog followed them into the room and sniffed at Mrs. Guidicatti's feet. Its hinder end was almost hairless and entirely coated with a soft tarry material. Mrs. Guidicatti looked down at it.

"Why! What happened to Midge?"

"Upset a kettle of boiling water on himself. There wasn't much of him before and there's less now. How's the city?"

"Cold. Devilish cold. We're going to take a vacation. What do you think of that? I'm just too mad."

"How so?"

Perrault and Guidicatti were coming in through the kitchen. Guidicatti was a little man. His forehead ran back in two points into his hair. His skin was dark and he wore a small black mustache. His wife said:

"I'm telling Mary how we have to take a vacation."

"Oh yes," said he in a slow gentle voice. "It's very annoying. It's on account of the union. I fiddled on Sunday in a cafeteria."

Mr. Guidicatti played the violin in the San Francisco Symphony Orchestra and his wife played the harp.

"What of that, what of that?" said Perrault, his voice sonorous and sudden. "Is it a blue law?"

"No, it's the union," said Guidicatti patiently. "They only let us work six days a week."

"What do you think of that?" said Mrs. Guidicatti. "They won't let a man work as he likes. They won't let him do anything. *A bas* the union. You can't call your teeth your own."

Perrault was getting out glasses and a bottle of red wine. The air was warm and full of the odor of cooking food.

"And these unions," said Mrs. Guidicatti, "anybody can belong to them that won't work! Musicians! They let people in that couldn't play 'Come to Jesus' on a barrel organ."

Perrault brought her a glass of wine. He was extremely handsome, very tall, his hair crisp and grizzled, having a decided wave. His nose started straight from the middle of his forehead with no dip between the eyes, the sort of nose technically known as Roman, but decidedly more Gallic than Roman. His eyes were dark and quick and his color ruddy.

He said, bowing, "Drown your sorrows, eh, Gemma. Let us forget the union."

She smiled, taking the glass, showing her teeth brightly.

"And the rabbits," she said. "How are the little rabbits?"

"Splendid," he said. "I have forty-two rabbits at the state fair, and I take forty-one prizes. Not so bad, eh?"

"And the little rabbit that didn't get a prize, he was very sad, I suppose?"

"You don't understand, Gemma. You don't understand how it happens."

Mrs. Perrault had gone into the kitchen. She stood by the coal range, stirring a fricassee. Guidicatti brought her a glass of wine. She didn't want it.

"Oh, come now. Just once. It won't do you a bit of harm."

"It won't do me a bit of harm not to, either."

"You always say the same thing."

"So do you."

He leaned against the doorjamb, drinking the wine himself, talking to his wife and Perrault in the one room and to Mary Perrault in the other. Outside the house the fields were dry and fragrant. About the distance of five blocks away were the railroad, a line of waving eucalyptus trees, a few houses, the edge of town. The meadow larks were singing. In the kitchen the big table was spread with a white cloth and set with plates and glasses. The sun winked in the empty dishes. The kitchen was snug. Through the open windows a cool dry spicy air blew in from the fields. Guidicatti sipped the wine and liked everything very much.

A little square-headed boy with white hair and brown eyes had followed the tarry dog into the room and was standing behind his mother now, keeping very still and well barricaded, and smiling unceasingly. When the three other children came in they all sat down to dinner. Chairs scraped. Everyone was talking. Mary Perrault stood by the stove dishing up rabbit fricassee and steamed summer squash. She passed the plates to one of the boys, who tilted back in his chair, taking them over his shoulder, and passed them on to the different places at the table. The little boy, Jamie, was sitting next to Mr. Perrault. He rubbed his head against his father's elbow. There were two older boys and a girl of about sixteen, Melanie. Jamie said something to Mr. Perrault.

"What did you say, my dear little son? My dear little son, you must learn to talk plainly," said Perrault in his rich French voice.

The child repeated his remark, rubbing his head along his father's arm.

"What did he say, Andrew?"

The oldest boy said lazily, "He said he made a wheelbarrow with a wheel and it worked." His face was dark and shrewd.

"Bravo, my dear little son, bravo."

"Aristide," said Mrs. Guidicatti to Mr. Perrault, "you have an accent like pea soup."

"The child has also an accent, that is all," added Guidicatti. "It is the accent of his own country. We do not live there."

Mrs. Perrault banged a pan on the stove and took her place at the table. They were very crowded. They began to eat at once.

Mary Perrault was perhaps forty years old. Her body was strong and rigid and thick, like the trunk of a tree. Her face was fresh, and a certain joyous tender look rose quickly into her eyes every so often. When Guidicatti saw this look he was always surprised that he had not noticed what a good-looking woman she was. She had the sort of face that has been scoured for generations by north wind, icy rain, and sea fog. Although she had been in California for twenty years you could see all the climate of Scotland by looking at Mary Perrault's face.

The dinner was very good. They ate a great deal, talking and laughing. They had another bottle of red wine, and when dinner was over Guidicatti smoked a cigar. They were all sitting around the table, leaning back in their chairs, or leaning forward with their elbows on the table. Guidicatti said, puffing at his cigar, extremely good-humored:

"Wouldn't you do well to have two more children in this family? Two nice little children, one four and one five, quiet and well behaved?"

"Oh, my dear God," said Perrault, "do you not really think we have enough trouble in this family as it is?"

"I have a friend," said Guidicatti, "a charming Frenchwoman."

"Yes, she is charming," said Mrs. Guidicatti.

"Her husband is not good to her," resumed Guidicatti, "so she is leaving him to earn her own living. Then she has the children to care for and she cannot take them with her. She can get a good job as a personal maid, without the children, but with the children—nothing. So she must find a good home for them, where she can pay to have them looked after."

"So they are French children, eh?" said Perrault.

"And Japanese," said Mrs. Guidicatti.

"Oh, my dear God," said Perrault, "what kind of a woman is that, to get a Japanese father for French children?"

"A very nice woman," said Mrs. Guidicatti, "just like you or me or anybody."

Melanie was interested. Mary Perrault said, "It would be too bad not to help her if she can't find anyone else to take them."

Perrault gave a magnificent snort, like a sea lion. Mrs. Guidicatti shook her napkin at him, and Mrs. Perrault began to clear the table.

Mr. Guidicatti went off with Perrault. The boys hung around the kitchen for a while with Melanie and the two women. They were teasing Melanie about her new fellow. She liked it. She sat on the table, swinging her legs and talking back to them in a strong loud voice. She had on a pale green dress of georgette, green kid shoes, and no stockings. The dress had no sleeves, but a very wide bertha fell across the upper arm. The wind blowing intermittently through the kitchen windows lifted the light stuff and showed the length of the arms, the skin bright with life.

"You're a disgraceful hussy," said Mrs. Guidicatti. "You don't wear any clothes and you have a new fellow every week. When are you coming up to see me?"

"Can't come till the season's over," said Melanie.

"What season?"

"At the cannery. Can't come until I have some money to spend."

"Well, we are going on a vacation next week. Vittorio

must go up the Russian River, for a place to go. From one cold place to a colder. But I tell you, Melanie, you should be careful. You are very pretty, and if you go around half naked all the time you will find yourself losing all moral restraint, and then you will catch horrible diseases. Your teeth will fall out, and you will lose your mind gradually, and die a horrible death."

"And Sodom and Gomorrah," said Mrs. Perrault, pouring scalding water into the dishpan. "Do you hear that, Melanie? Sodom and Gomorrah will be nothing to you."

"And you do not help your poor hard-working mother even with the dishes," wound up Gemma Guidicatti.

"Here's Jack," said Andrew. "Here's your fellow."

"Oh," said Melanie, running out of the room. She came back with her hat in her hand, a big-brimmed green straw. "Well, good-bye, Aunty Gemma, good-bye, Ma."

"Good-bye," said Mrs. Guidicatti. "I brought you a dress. It's in the front room. Be careful of horrible diseases."

"Thanks a lot. Good-bye." She went outdoors. The boys leaned out of the window, kidding her. Jack's car was making a great racket in the yard.

"Let me help you with the dishes now, Mary."

"No, no, you're not going to work today. Sit down in a chair and talk to me," said Mrs. Perrault.

"All right then. If I can't help, I'm going to fix this dress. The sleeves aren't right. Where's your workbasket?"

"In my room on the bed. Duncan, get it for your aunty Gemma."

He brought it to her, smiling and mocking. His hair was too long, growing down in soft blond points on his brown neck. He was very handsome, like his father, but not so dark. He had a soft downy muzzle.

"Now get out of here, the two of you," said Mrs. Guidicatti. "I want to take off my dress."

She shoved them out and shut the door.

"The worst of those children," she said to Mrs. Perrault, "is that they're just little Japs. To look at them you wouldn't think there was a drop of French blood in their bodies."

"Don't tell that to Perrault. That would be the end of their ever coming here."

"What made her marry him," said Mrs. Guidicatti, "it was just after the war, and he was in Paris. All her people were killed in the war and she hadn't a speck of money. At her age, and the way she was brought up, she didn't know what else to do. He's a perfect gentleman. I've met him. He's charming to meet."

She was sitting near the window. She had on a peacock-blue satin slip that made her bared arms and shoulders look very white. She bent her head over the sleeves she was ripping from the dress.

"What did he do to her to make her leave him?" said Mrs. Perrault.

"It was what he did to other women. She says he's always nice to her, but he's all the time going off with these Japanese women. I suppose it seems all right to him. She says if she could have it out with him she might be able to get along, but he won't fight with her. Just starts putting his arms around her and loving her this way and that. But you know," she said, puzzled, looking up from her work, "I think it's more the difference in physique. They weren't mated, you know. The races aren't built on the same scale."

Mrs. Perrault nodded. "Well," she said, "it's a strange business she should marry him, anyway."

"Yes, it is so," said Gemma.

Mrs. Perrault went on wiping dishes, and Mrs. Guidicatti, having ripped out both sleeves, basted them in again and tried the dress on. One looked very well. The other looked as bad as ever. She was having a hard time with it. She ripped the basting and tried again.

As she worked she said, "Guess what, I'm going to have a new harp."

They talked about cooking. Mrs. Perrault said, "A carrot in almost anything will make it taste so much sweeter. The little Italian woman next door, she puts a pinch of rosemary into almost everything she cooks."

Mrs. Guidicatti sewed and ripped. She said, "That harp is going to cost me seven hundred even."

"Imagine that," said Mrs. Perrault. "I can't imagine putting so much money into just a harp. Though Dad would put that much into a rabbit, if he could."

"It'll be worth it," said Mrs. Guidicatti, "in a financial way as well as artistically."

The men had spent the afternoon in the shade of the barn. Far away across the dry fields a line of sand-colored mountains with violet and air-blue shadows loomed through a curious silver haze. The fields seemed to be the floor of a level valley. In the opposite direction another line of hills, more massive, darker, wooded at the summits, rose, ridge by ridge, to be the barrier to the sea.

They talked about the union.

"With the rabbit business," said Perrault, "that is exactly what we need. If we would only stick together, it wouldn't be rabbits selling for something one year and for nothing the next, so you never know where you are. I have good rabbits. I have just about the best rabbits on the coast. Does that do me any good? No. For why? We don't stick together."

Guidicatti sighed deeply. He had a sympathetic nature, but he hated to belong to a union. These economic questions he was never sure about.

"Come and see my rabbits," said Perrault. "You never did see them all."

They walked among the hutches. Dinner had been late. They had wasted the afternoon without effort, and the air was dimming ever so faintly. The rabbits looked out at them with bright hard eyes. The little ones hopped about, making tiny soft thuds. Perrault opened the hutches and took out his prize rabbits, one after the other. There were brown ones, pure white ones, white ones hooded with black, gray ones.

"This fellow, he's my best buck," said Perrault, "and this fellow, he's a Blue Flemish. Look at him." He held the animal up by the nape of the neck, one hand under its feet. It was a gray, a gray so deep, so pure, so glossy that it was really blue, a wonderful color. "How do you like him?" said Perrault. "Here, lift him. He's a gentle one."

Guidicatti held out his hands, feeling slightly nervous and not wishing to appear so. He had never before touched a rabbit, that he could remember. Perrault put it into his hands slowly. The creature was very heavy, the fur warm under its surface coolness, under the fur the flesh, quivering, full of moving blood, little nerves, sinews. A meadow lark on the fence near them suddenly let out a burst of song. It was so sudden, so loud, so near, that Guidicatti felt as if he had touched the full throbbing throat. He felt in his hands the liveness of the rabbit, the song, the quivering warm breast of the lark. He was very startled and strangely alarmed. He gave the rabbit back to Perrault, who shut it into its dark box. All the way back to the house he felt it in his hands.

In the kitchen Mrs. Perrault was tying up boxes of eggs for them to take back to the city. There was also a basket of small dull yellow pears. She began to tell them as they entered:

"Gemma spent the whole afternoon remodeling her dress. She took both sleeves out and put them back in again inside out."

With the Spring

~~~~~~

THE HOUSE was a long, low, mulberry-
colored affair, rather shabby, standing far back on the
lot. A huge old oak leaned over it from the north, dropping long rigid branches on which the small dark leaves
were clotted like clusters of small birds. The grass, which
had been burnt over a few days previously, was partly
blackened ash and partly tawn, the black and the pale
straw color running into each other in strange designs.
Near the house along the sheltered south wall a row of
grapevines spread out their bright green leaves, the only
really vivid green in sight. On the front of the lot a small
new house stood in a plot of raw earth still splattered with
mortar, its walls freshly painted a light gray and shining
in the sunlight.

Between the old house and the new one a square two-
storied building which had once been a tank house for
the berry ranch did duty as a garage. It also was a mulberry color. The paint had been thinly applied a long
time ago, and now the grain of the wood was making
itself seen under the warm soft purple in little waves of
faint rosiny gold. The long, one-storied building and the

high square one made together a nice composition from almost any angle, a composition from which the little new house was excluded entirely, by its shape, its color, and the way it turned its back on the group.

A tea party was going on in the old house. The windows were open to the summer afternoon, and the ladies, glancing through them, could see on the one side the curtain of sparse oak boughs and on the other the trellis of bright leaves. A woman with a girlish face and drooping girlish figure sat near a window. She wore a white dress with a skirt much longer than was fashionable, and her hair, unfashionably arranged, was soft and fluffy with the softness of a child's. She was the owner and occupant of the new house, and the landlord of the old.

The hostess, a young woman, was passing sandwiches. She was a little embarrassed as she moved now here, now there with the plate, for her guests, except for the woman in white, were a good deal older than herself, prosperous, carefully dressed, and rather formal. One of them, a large woman with a delicately featured head, spoke of a plague of worms which had threatened the trees of the neighborhood a year or two before.

"They hung down everywhere from our oaks," she said, "and the poor trees! They were brown long before summer. I don't know what was the matter with the birds. They ought to have eaten them up."

The woman near the window nodded, resting the sandwich which she held in her hand against the edge of her teacup. "I remember," she said. "There wasn't a bird. I remember because it was the summer after my husband died. We always used to listen to the birds, and that summer there wasn't a bird. The oak tree was just pitiful. It looked so neglected." She smiled as she spoke. Her voice was gentle and hesitating, but quite self-possessed. She dropped the remark into the slight confusion and sunniness of the room as if it were the most natural remark in the world to make at a tea party.

The hostess paused, the plate in her hand, feeling a quiver of apprehension. Her emotion was half for her guest and half for the safety of her party. But nothing happened. The woman with the fine head said at once, "There are plenty of birds this year, the little scamps. They wake me up too early every morning." She added in explanation, "We have a rookery next door."

"Oh, rooks," said the woman in the white dress, and laughed.

A little later that same afternoon she said, "No, I don't think this was ever really a chicken house, though it looks like it. The chicken house is farther back on the lot. It was a berry ranch, this place, when we bought it, but my husband thought we could make a fortune out of chickens. My, the time and worry I spent over those chickens! I did everything for them except cure them of the gapes. I just couldn't do that. Eric had to do that for me." She paused and laughed, the same slight laugh as before, gentle, unembittered, humorous, although ever so faintly so. "I used to say to my husband, if I'd only spend half the energy in looking after you that I spend on those chickens, maybe you'd get well."

To the young woman at the tea table it seemed as if nothing could have been more tragic than that statement, and yet the tea party went on as before. Not a shadow fell into the room. Everyone seemed to take it as it was offered, a whimsical anecdote. Two of the ladies laughed, and the woman with the fine head smiled brightly, if briefly, and there was no knowing what echoes of sorrow it may have stirred in levels of the mind that have nothing to do with tea parties.

The day they had come to look at the house, the two young people, before renting it, Mrs. Norberg had told them the fact of her husband's death two years before, and that she meant to sell the new gray house as soon as she could build another. There was room for three or four more small houses on the big lot, and she thought that by subdividing and overseeing the building herself she could make enough money to get on her feet again. "He was sick three years before he died," she said, "and so there wasn't much left for us except the lot."

They walked up and down through the three empty rooms. It was too late for sunlight and too early for electricity. They opened and shut the small casement windows, looked in cupboards, asked about the stove, did it smoke, and each wondered what the other thought of it, not liking to ask openly in the presence of the small tired woman, who stood patiently, staring half forgetfully at the bare walls.

There were two children, a boy and a girl, both fair. The girl was little, a solid, sweet child, like an apple, but without the wild fragrance that an apple has. The boy gave them a start because he was beautiful, as a girl might be, although thoroughly a boy. In the evening, the day after they moved in, the children had piled rubbish for a bonfire, and after supper the ruddy flickers entered the kitchen and played upon the smooth painted walls and shut doors of the cupboards. The new tenants went outside and crossed the dark ground toward the fire.

Mrs. Norberg was sitting there with the little girl at her side. The boy kept wandering about the edge of the light, bringing more fuel or stamping out the sparks that sometimes flamed in the dry grass. The light caught on his hair and small, fresh features, and the dirty white corduroy trousers. The fire thickened the darkness, leaving visible only the people and the branches of the oak tree, illumined from below, and established a sort of intimacy. They were all very tired.

Mrs. Norberg said, "It seems as if moving's the most endless job. I've been moving into the new house ever since two weeks ago, and everything's still upside down. My husband had so many books, math books, he was a mathematics teacher, and books are the worst things in the world to move. They get so dirty and they're so heavy. And now nobody wants them. I hate to pack his things away, but there just isn't room for them. They're all going to have to go into boxes in the garage. I'm going to save them for Eric, though he probably won't want to be a mathematician at all. He wants to be an artist. Like me. I always wanted to paint, I always meant to, until after I was married. Well, we can't do everything in this life."

She spoke with long pauses between the sentences, and yet with a certain little quick rush in the words themselves. These were confidences, amenities, not complaints. They stirred her, made her seem youthful, and like her son.

Yet sometimes the younger woman would see her moving about in the garden, her skirt muddied and her shoulders drooping, dragging the heavy hose, or coming at dusk from the corn patch at the far end of the lot, her head fallen forward, watching the hard path, and she would think of figures in Daumier's drawings of the poor. Her voice, if she spoke at these times, was drained, and her features drained in the same way by a limitless fatigue. It was not actually the fatigue of labor. She was like a fountain, sinking back into this exhaustion as a stream of rising water shrivels and shrinks into nothing.

Days when the sun shone richly on the weathered, reddish walls of the house, and the grape leaves, tilting this way and that as if under the weight of the sunlight, broadened, and the green waxy clusters which they sheltered grew larger, the young woman in the house was very happy. Over the back porch was a rose vine with small bronzy leaves and little pink many-petaled flowers. They cast a spicy sweetness about the back door, over the beds of chard and pieplant, and their soft pink was beautiful against the mulberry. Going in and out, hanging wet washing on the line, taking empty cans and bottles to the trash box in the garage, pulling weeds from the vegetable bed, she reflected that the relativity of time, of the different times existing simultaneously on different moving objects, is no stranger than the relativity of lives. Trivial happiness, the most precious kind of all, existed in her, and had a right to, and yet she was daily aware of Mrs. Norberg's sorrow.

Eugenia Norberg had cased the windows in the red house herself. She had also paneled the living room with building board, the children helping her, and her husband, lying on the cot in the corner, watching them all with great amusement. With the first pieces in place the room had suddenly indicated how nice it was going to be. "Like an attic on the ground," she said, "a studio attic." She was pleased. A little flush came into her cheeks, and she shoved her loosened hair back of her ear with a quick gesture. Eric was measuring the next panel.

"Be sure and get it straight," she said.

He gave her a small, mischievous look over his shoulder. "Straight, Mother, or straight with the house?"

His father laughed. The little girl, who was making biscuits in the kitchen, came in to see what he was laughing about, and they repeated the joke to her. She did not laugh, but stood bright-eyed and interested, a big blue-and-white checked apron tied around her neck, flour on her hands, and a streak of it on her chin. It was one of those days when they all believed that he was going to get well in a year or two, and then they would go back to Idaho, to the small university town, the rolling hills, the pheasants crossing the roads as they drove out into the country, the rains, the cold sweet air. The children still wrote letters to children there with whom they had gone to school.

Then the conviction, growing from day to day, denied by all of them from day to day, that he was not going to get well. Then the death, the service from the Lutheran church in town, and the return to the house. Mrs. Norberg was haunted by a delusion which she well recognized as such. "In Idaho everything was all right, he was with us. Here in California we are alone and he is dead. If we could go back to Idaho it would be like going back into past time and he would be with us there again, and alive."

But for lack of money she was tied to the red house, the chickens, and the berry patch. The chief value of her land lay in the rapid growth of the nearby town. In three years, or in five years, it would be worth a good deal. So the thought of moving was set aside indefinitely.

The funeral was on a Saturday. Monday morning she sent the children back to school. It was winter, and a foggy day. She looked through the closed window to the branches of the oak tree, dimly drawn upon a background of untransparent gray. She took her workbasket and a pile of mending into the front room and sat there. She could feel the mist pressing against the house, and the rooms were empty. There was not even a cat. She was tired, with a bodily fatigue to which she paid little attention because of the anguish in her mind. The emotion was tangible. It was in her mind, in her body, and in the air. When she lifted a sock and slipped it over her left hand she lifted it through anguish, a substance. The sock had a big hole at the side of the heel. The edges were badly frayed. She wondered if there was a bit of rough leather in one of Eric's shoes to cause it. She slipped the needle into the material, catching the cloth up in little stitches until the tiny shining length was barred evenly with dark. It was a bad hole, but when she had finished the neat basket weave of thread the space was filled and the sock was not puckered anywhere. She bit off the end of darning cotton and lifted her head. She had forgotten in this trivial concentration the fog, the grief, the events of the last four days. Now with the sight of the familiar walls reflecting the grayness of the fog the anguish returned suddenly, doubled, drowning her, infinitely more dreadful for the slight respite she had had. She almost screamed.

She did not say to herself in so many words, "I must never forget again, even for one second," but she braced

herself against forgetting, and told over to herself
minutely the whole unbearable event.

Spring came slowly on. The children at first were a
little shy before their mother's sorrow. They differentiated
sharply, unintentionally, between their grief and hers.
Their own they could manage, hers they could not. But
when she began to speak of their father's death in connection with some quite trivial household thing, or remembering some joke they all had in common, as if the
death were not an unnamable mystery but part of their
common life from then on, their embarrassment was dis-
solved, they breathed more easily and dared to go on
about the business of being happy.

In the next lot, between the kitchen garden and the
chicken houses, a strip of orchard began to bloom, the
most sheltered trees first, and then the delicate white
conflagration running from tree to tree, hiding the limber
branches. Or, "like popcorn," the little girl said. The air
was tender, with a quality like legend, somehow far off
and gentle. One day Mrs. Norberg saw Eric climbing the
oak tree by the house. She was working in the garden,
on her knees on the damp earth. She sat back on her
heels, letting the trowel drop beside her, and followed
him with her eyes. All the oaks grew with a heavy south-
ward slant, induced by the century-long pressure of the
wind blowing down from the bay. The boy walked up
the trunk on his hands and toes. Above the height of the
roof a branch went out horizontally. He crept along it
and seated himself astride of it, busy at untying a rope
which he had hung there the autumn before. His motions were light and accurate, and, seated there so high,
he seemed to be riding the air. His mother was struck

with his happiness, the simple happiness of being alive and able. She thought of her grief at her husband's death and of her son's happiness, a happiness which was also hers, and neither emotion impaired the other. They were coexistent, and she had so disciplined herself during the late winter and early spring never to forget the one that it was impossible to consider the other by itself. She was still afraid that joy, unmixed with grief, would vanish like a mirage. But this day she understood that by re-membering, by holding all her life steadily before her, she could maintain a joy also in all its proper quality. She reached for the trowel, and when her hand found it, it rested there without lifting the tool. Eric came down from the tree and disappeared around the corner of the house, coiling his rope as he went.

She looked at the fresh earth in front of her, which, soft and ready to receive the roots of plants, was like a thought, a statement only of itself. She read it over and over, and let her mind slide from her, and lie upon the spring air. They were building the frame of a house about the distance of a block away. The blows were muted and mellowed, and carried the sense of unfinished wood, rafters and beams, and curled shavings. When she was partly rested she lifted the trowel and dipped it in the earth.

Summer came, hot, dry, and hazy. She planned the new house and built it, and at the beginning of the next summer she rented the red house and moved. Sometimes her tenant came to borrow something or return it. She watched the young woman picking her way between the newly set-out whips of rosebushes in the back yard, and, standing at the back door with the returned article in her hands, Mrs. Norberg found herself gossiping a little.

Sometimes, "Oh, I take my housework easy. I have a house to live in, not to make me miserable," she said. "The man that undertook to build this house for me was scandalized by the cobwebs in the old house. Maybe you've noticed, it's just about impossible to keep the spiders out of it. So I let them spin. He said, 'You'll take so much more of an interest in your new house, Mrs. Norberg. You'll enjoy working around in it.' I said, 'If I'm going to do that I won't build it.'" Or they would talk of a neighbor who was ill, and she might say, "It's hard for a young person to be sick. If it was me I wouldn't care. I don't really care whether I live any more or not. I often think of my husband. It seems such a pity that he had to die. He wanted so much to live. He was young, in that way." Or another time, "I sometimes say to myself, 'I've nothing more to go on for,' and then I say, 'But of course, I've got the children!'"

She looked down at the face of her tenant and saw friendliness and interest, and knew that she was not imposing her tragedy upon her listener, in spite of what her words might say. She felt sometimes, while talking casually like this, a sort of spiritual resilience within herself, and she thought less of the fatigue that followed it.

So she went on, with the spring, with summer, with the children's happiness, carrying always a grief which did not diminish with the passing of days, but adding to it, somehow, from time to time, a sort of joy, a sort of graciousness, as one might welcome a guest into a house already crowded and entertain him courteously.

Apricot Harvest

~~~~~~

THE CHILDREN hopped off the truck and began to swarm into the cutting shed, surrounding Mrs. Larsen, fifteen or twenty of them—the truck had been jammed—all grammar school boys and girls in blue jeans and striped jellybean shirts. Save that the girls rolled their jeans up below the knee and tied bright colored handkerchiefs about their heads, they were dressed just like the boys. A few mothers followed slowly. These were Arne's workers. He went all the way to Redwood City for them, and every afternoon at three-thirty he took them all home again. It was the best he could do. All the local help—what there was of it, this summer of 1944—was already engaged in the bigger orchards. But this was Arne's first big year. This year he had not only his own orchard to harvest, but he had rented two others in the hills, and every tree in every orchard all up and down the valley was loaded with apricots as never before in the memory of anyone he knew.

Last year, just home from the agricultural college at Davis, he had built the sulphur house and the cutting shed, prepared to do things in the right way; and there had been no 'cots. No more than he could handle by himself. The spring rains had come at just the wrong moment, as the fruit was setting, and the brown rot had got nearly every blossom at the core.

But this year—this year he had already seen branches broken with the weight of the fruit, and he had put props under some of his trees as if they had been prune trees.

Under the shed Arne's mother, Mrs. Larsen, was checking boxes for the children; a forty-cent punch on the score card with a box of firm fruit, a fifty-cent punch with a box of soft fruit. Sometimes it took a box and a half to fill a tray; the cutters were paid by the tray, and whoever started with a soft box was obliged to stick it out with the soft fruit until the last small corner of the tray was filled.

Mrs. Larsen was a large woman. She wore a white cotton hat perched on top of her short gray hair and a large blue apron tied squarely about her waist. She moved about the shed slowly and awkwardly because the varicose veins in her legs gave her pain, and her face was lined and bleached with age. Nevertheless her smile was charming. It had a lovely, girlish quality, a little hesitant, a little coaxing, and she looked at the children inquiringly with her mild blue eyes that needed no spectacles.

"Dey dat comes early gets de best fruit," she said. "Today we got nice fruit. Arne yoost brought it in from de hill orchard. Hare now," she interrupted herself, laying a hand on the arm of one of the girls. "You are too liddle to be lifting dat box. Arne vill take it over for you." She punched the card, read the name on it again, and smiled as she hung it about the child's neck. "And you," she said in surprise to a small, black-eyed boy with a clipped head, "you want soft fruit today when we got such nice 'cots? You going to be rich. Look at all dose fifty-cent punches you got already on your card! You work good, I guess."

The children scattered to the far corners of the shed, and with them went a spirit of festival. It was too early in the day for them to be unruly. They were still feeling gay, fresh, and obedient. It was a beautiful day, the wind blowing from the bay with just enough coolness to temper the July heat, and the scent of apricots was a fragrance, not too sweet. The few women who were already at work and the one old man looked up as the children surrounded them. The women smiled, and the old man said without smiling, "Don't jostle," but their arrival seemed somehow to ally the apricot cutting with the great and joyous harvest festivals of time past, and everyone was suddenly aware that it was indeed a beautiful day. And since most of the people working there were neighbors or friends of the Larsens, who had come to help Arne "make a crop," people who would not have been helping in another year, the occasion had its resemblance to the barn raisings and quilting bees of an earlier generation.

"Arne sold the whole crop to the government," somebody said. "It's going overseas. He's going to dry it all."

Arne, in building his cutting shed, had not considered the principles of dynamic symmetry, but he had nevertheless managed to give this floorless structure with its pillars of four-by-fours and its wide pitched roof, some of the grace and dignity of the Parthenon. Save on the

side where the driveway approached it, the shed was surrounded by orchard, the small sturdy trees stretching
away in even files, at right angles to the sides, wheeling
obliquely at the corners, filling every view completely, a
world beginning and ending in trees. And every tree
among its thick green leaves held forth the heavy clusters
of golden balls. Under the trees the earth was soft and
bare. Arne had set out the drying trays on the eastern
side of the shed, each tray set overlapping slightly the
edge of the tray beside it, so that each had a sunward
slant, each, in the distance, an even patch of delicate,
roseate orange.

On one side of the driveway stood the sulphur house,
and on the other side a huddle of shrubbery hid the
chicken shed, the garage, and, beyond them, the small
house in which Arne lived with his mother.

Mrs. Larsen checked the last of the children and took
a turn about the shed, slowly and painfully, to see that
everything was going smoothly. The children had teamed
up, two to a tray, except the ambitious small boy with
the dead-ripe fruit. He was attempting the big tray
singlehanded. Mrs. Larsen smiled at him, and remarked
that Mrs. Hergesheimer and Mrs. Antonio were almost
ready for new trays, emptied a can of pits for Mrs. John-
son, and found herself back near the driveway entrance
to the shed. Here she encountered a woman whose face
was familiar but whose name she did not know. She was
a small, tidily built woman of middle age, with a small,
tight, tidy face, and she had come prepared with her
apron on and a sharp paring knife in her hand. Her expression was pleasant; she looked efficient and friendly,
and her bright gray eyes roamed with amusement over

APRICOT HARVEST 95

the scene behind Mrs. Larsen, but for some reason which
she did not understand the sight of her affected Mrs.
Larsen very unpleasantly.

Just then Arne opened the door to the sulphur house,
and, with the aid of an older man, ran the load of trays
out upon the narrow track, a pile higher than his head,
and heavy. With the opening of the doors came a whiff
of sulphur smoke. It blew past the women and dissi-
pated itself quickly.

"You want to cut?" inquired Mrs. Larsen, raising her
voice a little as the men trundled the load of trays past
them.

The woman nodded. "If I can be of any help. You
don't remember me, do you?"

"Sure, I remember you," said Mrs. Larsen. This was
at least half the truth. She remembered the face, and
there was something associated with it that made her feel
ill; and yet she was clear in her mind that the woman
herself was not the source of the feeling. She did not wish
to hurt the feelings of anyone who was willing to help
Arne make his crop. So she smiled and said: "People iss
so nice to help Arne. I don't know how he would make
out dis year widout de neighbors help so much." This
seemed to be the right thing to say. It had the right
effect. "I help you set up a tray. You ever cut before?"

No, she never had, but she helped Mrs. Larsen steady
the big tray, as big as an average door, upon the trestles,
and gave her a hand with the box of apricots. The fruit
rolled out on the darkened boards, dark as if resinous
with the sap of other years. Mrs. Larsen set an empty
coffee can to receive the scraps of marred fruit, and another for the pits.

"We save all de pits," she said. "We sell 'hem to a place in 'he city, and dey make dis paste for macaroons out'n 'hem. Isn't dat funny? And dey safe all 'he shells and make charcoal for gas masks."

She was full of admiration for the economy of things. She picked up an apricot of firm, pale gold, faintly reddened and freckled on one cheek, and slit it neatly round on the natural line of indentation. The fruit parted smoothly, the dry pit fell out, and Mrs. Larsen carefully set the cleft halves like little golden dishes side by side on the edge of the tray. The other woman followed her example. She was a natural-born cutter, Mrs. Larsen could see, and was going to need no instructions. But who was she?

"You wouldn't dare," said a young voice behind her. Turning, Mrs. Larsen found almost beside her the ambitious little boy who had undertaken the tray of dead-ripe fruit. The voice came from across the shed. The little boy balanced in his hand an apricot that was so soft, so full of juice that it no longer had a shape, but was merely an unbroken sack that shifted the weight of its contents as the boy rolled it about on the palm of his uplifted hand. It needed no mind reader to deduce his intentions. The little girl across the shed repeated, "You wouldn't dare," and Mrs. Larsen gently removed the apricot from the boy's hand. She smiled down into his surprised face.

"You mustn't waste de good fruit," she said in mild reproof. "Dis is de best, de sweetest." She cut it, and with her clumsy-seeming, skillful hands arranged the halves so that the juice should not run out of the skins.

"Slabs, dey call dese ones," she said to the boy, "but yoost de same, dey is de sweetest."

She turned back to her own tray.

"It's nice here under the shed," said the woman, ranging her line of halved apricots. "The shed wasn't built, the last time I was here. It makes things look different."

"Yah," said Mrs. Larsen. "It's much better de girls don't have to stand in de sun so long. Sometimes dey used to get headaches; and it makes de fruit hot. De smell gets strong and some of de liddle girls gets sick from de smell. Yah, it sure makes t'ings look different."

She smiled in pride at Arne's improvements, and then, quite suddenly, with no teasing half revelations, but completely, she remembered when she had last seen this woman, she remembered her name and where she lived and all the details of that day, now almost six years gone. It was strange that she should have forgotten, even briefly; and then again, it was not strange, for the face was so small a part of the events of that day. Indeed, things looked different. It was strange that there could be two such days in the life of anyone, that day and this; strangest of all that this present day should have arisen almost to blot out that—to blot it out as full morning sunlight blots out the night of terror.

It was the day after her brother-in-law's funeral. So rainy the day had been, the trees bare of their leaves, the long drifts of wet leaves lying by the side of the drive under the walnut trees. The white-painted sulphur house and the spacious shape of the cutting shed gone from the picture, the house and garage and the chicken houses seemed small and dark and old and lost in the shrubbery. The orchard was not as thriving to behold then as now, either, and the rain had dragged the chrysanthemums low to the uncut grass. The death of her brother-in-law had been sudden, giving her sister no time to prepare her mind or her house. Mrs. Larsen had spent the day after the services with her sister, trying to put the house in order. Her sister had been very brave, indeed she had, but still she had needed company and help. Mrs. Larsen had given up her day with the sick old woman whose house she cared for and whose bed she changed three times a week and had gone to help her sister. A death and a funeral turn a whole house upside down. It had been a beautiful funeral with many white and purple asters and many yellow chrysanthemums, and a friend had sung the Swedish hymns in such a beautiful voice that it made her think of her father and mother and the spring twilight prolonged above the sea beyond Öland. Her husband had said that it was a beautiful service. While she stood beside him, weeping and blowing her nose, he had stood tearless and very dignified, but afterward he had praised the service to her and to Inge.

So she came home on the bus and had to walk from the bus stop home through the rain, and she came down the long driveway to the house in the early dark, feeling very tired. She could ill afford that year to give up her day with the old woman, but one has to do what one can for one's own people. Her husband had been out of work again. First there had been no work—for years, it seemed, no work worthy of the name. He had even gone East for a while, but the job had not lasted. Then he had come home. The whole country seemed so bitter and sad, as if there were never going to be good times again. Then slowly the times got better, and Mr. Larsen got a job, but he did not get over the bitterness of the bad years. It seemed as if he had been bitter and gloomy too long. So when he smashed his thumb and had to quit the job again, because it was fine work—printer's work—and he had to use all his fingers, he said it was beginning all over again. Again his wife would have to work to keep the family. Again he was out of a job because, when there was work to be done, was anyone going to keep a job open for him until his hand got better?

When she came to the end of the drive, where it turned toward the garage, she saw how dark and small the house looked. There was no light in the windows and the twilight, shining on the wet wood, showed it to be darkened by the rain. The paint was so nearly gone, the water clung to the wood. There was a great sadness in her heart for Inge, and she wished also that she had been able to do the day's work and had the little roll of four dollars in her pocketbook.

The boys had not come home for their uncle's funeral. There were only her husband and herself in the house. Still, dark as it was, and empty, since her husband seemed to have gone out, and cold, with no fire left in the stove, the house gave her a sense of comfort as she entered the kitchen. The last two days had been like a journey into a strange land. Now, as she switched on the light, and built up a fire, hung up her wet coat and filled the coffeepot with water at the wooden sink, she felt a sort of gratitude to the stove, the coffeepot, the small, crowded house.

It had only two rooms—the kitchen and the other room. Since the kitchen was too small to hold a cot, the boys, when they were home, slept on the porch. It was

not until she took the coffee cups to the table that she
found the letter, weighted down by the salt and pepper
boxes, in the middle of the table. It was written in pencil.
It was hard to read, and she read it through once with
all her attention on deciphering the words before the
sense of the words themselves reached her.

DEAR WIFE,
*I am sorry to do this. It seems no use to go on. When
you open the chicken house be sure there is someone
with you. There will be fumes.*

The sense came through to her at first very slowly, the
separate words themselves on the limp, lined paper being
so hard to understand. Then, in a flood of understanding,
she knew about the fumes in the chicken house, and since
there was no hour indicated on the note, and no thought
of the hour entered her mind, she thought that she must
prevent him, and, dropping the paper, she ran from the
kitchen, stumbling, into the rain and the thickening
twilight. Outside the chicken house, in the yard, the
hens were huddled against the wall; someone had closed
the doorways to the nests. They stirred as she approached,
and came running and fluttering against the wire, cluck-
ing and squawking. She tried to open the door to the
chicken house, but it did not give at her pull. It had been
fastened from the inside. She ran her hand up and down
the door; she beat upon the door with the flat of her
hand and called her husband by name.

"Open 'he door, open 'he door," she called. "Quick,
quick, open 'he door."

But no one answered. At a little break in the wood
she was able to push her finger in, and the nail scraped

upon something taut and hollow. She recognized it for paper pasted over the crack. He had sealed it. She knew it all, now. They had fumigated last summer against vermin. With cyanide. She knew all about sealing the cracks.

"Open 'he door! Quick, quick!" she shouted again in sharper terror. There was a commotion among the hens, as the hardier ones pushed to be closer to the wire, but inside the chicken house everything was still. Then, as she realized the finality of the moment, she was no longer a suppliant toward a man who hardened his will against her distress and would not reply; she was only an old woman standing alone in the rain. She looked beside her and behind her, as if there should have been someone with her, but she was quite alone. There were wet bushes beside her, and the shallow puddles shining in the driveway, and the rain falling in the half-darkness between the orchard trees as far as she could see. She had never in her life felt so completely alone.

She remembered then that he had told her, in the letter, to have someone with her when she opened the chicken house, and obediently she turned down the driveway, walking through the rain without remembering to stop for her coat, walking down to the main road. She went to the nearest house, and, although it was the nearest, she had never before been within the iron fence. She walked up the unfamiliar driveway, past the low bushy palm tree, past the front door, around to the back, because there was a light there, and the woman who came to answer her knock was Mrs. Hoskings, the woman with the tidy, pleasant face who was now cutting apricots at the same tray with her. A man had gone back

with her. Mrs. Hoskings had stayed to telephone for a
doctor and for Inge. She had hardly seen Mrs. Hoskings
since. That was why she had not remembered her.

She set the halves of the apricot down gently and
raised her eyes cautiously to the face of the woman across
from her. She was prepared to smile if Mrs. Hoskings
looked at her, but Mrs. Hoskings was busy with the
fruit, her face calm and happy. She was not thinking
about that rainy night.

Inge had come; she had been indignant. She had held
that Mr. Larsen had no right to end his life; it had not
belonged to him but to others. His wife had defended
him. After all, she had been close to him through all
those years of discouragement. It would have been
stupid of her, as well as unkind, not to understand. Late
that night they had talked about it, and the next morning, wedged into the little kitchen, between the table
and the wall, between the table and the stove, while
they waited for the boys, Mrs. Larsen and her sister had
talked about it all again.

"I tell you," said Inge, "what it was. He was yoost
yealous of my husband. Lots of times in 'e last years it's
been worse. He had to go and choose 'he day after my
husband's funeral." She spread out her hands on the
table, white hands with tapering fingers, the broad gold
ring shining on the wedding finger, hands that had
worked hard but were still white.

Mrs. Larsen looked down at her sister's hands, feeling that her sister was younger than she was, that her
very indignation was a sign of her being younger. She
herself accepted the tragedy. She accepted the deser-
tion and could not bring herself to blame that very sad

and bitter man. Yet then, and many times later, she said to herself, "How he could leave the boys!" And indeed times had been worse than this last year. Perhaps it was as Inge thought: he had been seized with envy of the dead. After all, he had said to her that it had been a beautiful funeral.

There was a prolonged rumbling as Arne ran the first load of cut fruit down the track to the sulphur house. His mother lifted her head and looked after him as one looks, slightly dazzled, who has come from within a darkened room. Arne leaned against one corner of the load, and against the other corner a slender, white-haired man, bared to the waist and brown as leather, leaned and pushed with all his might. Mrs. Larsen did not know his name. He was, she knew, a retired professional man of some sort who had come to help in order that the fruit might not go to waste. Arne, in blue denim jacket and pants, turned, shifting his other shoulder to the load, and his mother could see how blue his eyes were in the tan of his face. He was laughing, and to his mother he looked triumphant as well as gay.

She passed a hand across her eyes. Somehow the two days, the day of despair and this day, so bright around her, fell into a natural relationship. She did not know how things could have changed so greatly; she was too humble to take credit to herself for all her work and patience. She thought of how the world was all at war, of Arne's older brother almost beyond the reach of letters in the western sea, but for the moment the thing she understood best was that all the bare and empty branches of that rainy night stood now filled with leaves and fruit.

People Don't Want Us

~~~~~~

KATHRYN DOUGLASS watched the children go down the road to meet the yellow school bus, saw them climb on board, and so depart from her jurisdiction for the next six or seven hours. It was a lovely morning, March in California. There were new blossoms here and there in the thick new green of the yellow jasmine. Across the road the apricot orchard was on the verge of blossoming, all the twigs ruddy with new sap and swollen with the shapes of buds still sheathed in their deep red. In a day or two it would all seem white and snow-laden.

Mrs. Douglass traversed her grassy lawn, paused at the door long enough to break a long spray from the yellow jasmine, and returned to her disordered living room. The floor was woolly with lint; the dust was so thick on the piano that it could be pushed up in rolls with a finger; newspaper littered the floor, the chairs, the sofa. Standing there, with the long yellow-blossomed spray drooping from her hand, Mrs. Douglass surveyed confusion, and the depression which she felt was not all due to the lack of house cleaning. Related to it, yes, but not caused by it.

For a week now she had been saving up the dust for Mrs. Larsen, who was to have come this morning and gathered it all up, and presented Mrs. Douglass with rooms so clean that she could ignore the thought of dust again until the following Thursday. But this morning at eight o'clock Mrs. Larsen had phoned that she was ill with the flu. Mrs. Douglass was trying to finish a story, and she had counted heavily upon having this day to herself, at least until the hour when the children returned from school. But Mr. Douglass was bringing strangers home to dinner, and it was for once imperative that the dust be removed at least from the living room. But if she began upon the living room the rest of the house would demand similar attention, and there was a company dinner to be prepared besides. The story would be shot. It added up rather badly, so badly in fact that Mrs. Douglass had hunted up a long-unused telephone number and had phoned Anna. Would Anna come, for friendship, and clean house for her? She did not like to ask her to come so far. Since they had moved from the old place, she had seen Anna only on special occasions, such as the day before Christmas, or the day before Thanksgiving, and sometimes on a Sunday afternoon at the height of the strawberry season. The small faraway voice with the foreign accent had replied that Anna would be happy to come. She would come right away.

Mrs. Douglass picked up the funny sheet from the floor where Billy had been enjoying it, picked up the main news section from her husband's chair, and began to restore the paper to something like its former coherence. She spread it out on the table, laying the spray of yellow jasmine temporarily beside it, and took a quick look at the headlines. As usual, that spring, they were bad. This was that spring when it became more and more apparent each day that the men at Bataan and on Corregidor were expendable, that they were being abandoned, that no help was going to be sent to them in spite of the hopes held out from day to day. There were also the usual items about the approaching evacuation of the Japanese from the West coast. Harriet's boy was in the Philippines, somewhere. A lot of the boys from Salinas had been sent there, and he was with them. Harriet was no older than she was, but had married earlier, and her first child had been a boy. So that now he was at Bataan. Billy, through an accident of time, was going to escape this war. But it was only an accident. It might just as well have been Billy who was out there.

She folded the paper. She had an impulse to hide it, before it should reach Anna's eyes, and she looked about for a place in which to put it where it might be less conspicuous. But in the end she laid it on the table, just as she usually did. After all, Anna Yoshida could read English. She was not like her old mother, who still could neither read nor speak the new language. And whether she could read the papers or not, she knew perfectly well that she had become an enemy in their midst, willy-nilly, on that Sunday morning last December.

Mrs. Douglass had gone with Billy and Marion before Christmas with gifts for all the Yoshidas, as usual, except that among Christmas preparations greatly reduced by the excitement of being at war and the making of blackout curtains, the gifts for the Yoshidas were nicer than usual, for a purpose, in order to say, "You have not become barbarians for us overnight." The winter rains had, as usual, surrounded the small unpainted house with a quarter acre of black adobe mud. Beyond the mud the rows of celery plants stretched orderly and green, but the big field in which the strawberries used to grow had been let go to weed. The Yoshidas were not at home. The place was as deserted as if the temporary absence were symbolical of the long absence to come. Everyone knew then that "something would have to be done about the Japanese."

They left the presents by the front door, hoping that the rain would not whip under the porch and spoil the pretty wrappings; they scraped the gumbo from their shoes as best they could before climbing back into the car, and drove, rather sadly, away.

A short distance down the road they passed the old place, and the children, who could not remember it very well, looked at it curiously, while their mother noted further changes, consisting mostly of the absence of familiar trees or shrubs. The removal of the rose hedge across the front of the lawn made the place look neater, it was true. The bushes had been breaking down the old wire fence with their weight. But how sweet they had been in early April, the two scented pink ones, the two scentless and thornless, and the one deep damask red! They had all been so happy at the old place that Kathryn Douglass sometimes wondered why they had left it. Then she had to remind herself that it was too close to the bay, that the children woke with bronchial coughs from the low-lying winter fogs, and that the fields round about had been deep in mud and water during the winter

months, like the Yoshidas' front yard. Of course the new
place on the higher ground was much pleasanter, but
she still regretted her old neighbors. She regretted the
Yoshidas.

It was not that she was exactly intimate with the
Yoshidas. Far from it. But there had been built up
through the years a tenuous bond, even an affection, it
seemed to Kathryn Douglass, made of experiences shared
—weather and work, fear, loss, happiness, and the children. Perhaps she was fond of the Yoshidas only because
they had been a part of the children's earliest years. At
any rate, she never drove down the road past the old
place without a pang of homesickness and regret; and
now that she stood looking down at the morning paper,
blackened with so much disaster and hate, she felt a
great desire to protect Anna Yoshida from the actions of
her race, from the weight of the times which had so little
to do with Anna, or with Kathryn Douglass, or with the
children playing on the grass at the old place.

It had all begun, as she remembered, the day that the
cat had left home with the four new kittens. She had not
left to stay, but, as Marion had said, had only taken them
down the road to see the paper goldfish. It would have
been a most natural thing to do, for in the yard beside
the newly erected frame house down the road two poles
had been set up, and from a rope stretched between the
poles floated, or leaped, or subsided, according to the
wind, five magnificent paper kites, in the form of carp.
The wind entered at their round open mouths and puffed
them out to splendid dimensions. The longest must have
been six feet, the smallest at least four. The sun glistened
upon the gold crosshatching of their scales, vermilion,

orange, blue, black, green, and on the round circles of their eyes.

It was May, the fifth of May, and the air was balmy, the wind not too erratic. The locust trees at the Dutchman's house had been in bloom, and their fragrance had swept the fields. Marion had followed the cat, and her mother had followed Marion. Marion wanted a fish kite. Marion was three? Or was she four years old? Her mother had to pause and calculate.

They had known that the Dutchman had leased his acres to some Japanese on a five-year lease, and they had watched the frame house being put up, unpainted, very simple, a child's plan of a house, but they had not yet spoken with any of the new arrivals. To please Marion, Mrs. Douglass had gone in search of the owner of the kites. They had found Anna on her knees in the strawberry field.

A small figure in blue trousers bound close about her ankles, wearing an old-fashioned cotton sunbonnet with a ruffle at the back to cover her neck, Anna rose from her work and came to meet them. With one hand she pushed back her bonnet and wiped the sweat from her face. She had need to push back the bonnet to look up at the tall woman who was interrupting her. In her other hand she held the box into which she had been packing berries. The hand was brown and very small.

Mrs. Douglass inquired about the kites. Anna shook her head. She explained. The kites belonged to her son, a first son in the Yoshida family. No, it was not his birthday, but this was Boy Day, and on Boy Day the boy's friends and well-wishers give him fish kites. These fish are the carp who do not like to live in muddy water, but

who are always trying to swim upstream. They are given
to a boy on Boy Day in order to teach him to be like the
carp, to seek pure water and a pure life and to swim upstream. They are not given to girls.

Marion took in the fact that fish kites were not for
girls and looked disappointed. Anne was sorry but firm.
She offered strawberries to Marion, and Marion was
consoled. Of Mrs. Douglass she inquired:

"Do you have a boy?"

Mrs. Douglass shook her head, feeling meanwhile the
pride in this small brown woman before her that she did
indeed have a boy, and a first son. Anna said, very kindly
and yet a little shyly:

"When you have a boy, we will bring you kites on
Boy Day."

It was a promise, and when it was made Mrs. Douglass
had no way of knowing that it would ever be fulfilled.
And yet when, after the lapse of years, Billy had been
some eight months in this world, the Yoshidas appeared
on the fifth of May, the promise was kept, and two kites,
one black and gold, one gold and vermilion, flew over
the Douglasses' grass plot. In the meantime, what had
the Douglasses actually come to know of the Yoshidas?
Very little, perhaps. What mattered was the way they
felt about the Yoshidas.

The next winter Anna came one day a week and
helped Mrs. Douglass with the laundry and the house
cleaning. It had been a piece of luck for Mrs. Douglass,
for the old place was so far from the end of the bus line
that none of the charwomen from the town would consider coming there. And Anna took up so little space
around the house. She was quiet and conscientious and

cheerful. Kathryn Douglass was distinctly grateful to her. Then, as the winter approached spring, Anna excused herself. She now had to help in the fields. From the distance, as she drove down the road, Kathryn Douglass saw her figure, bent low to the ground, weeding, planting, cultivating, in the last cold foggy mornings of February, in the wet days of March. "The mud never sticks to the Japanesers' feet," was the saying down the road. When other people said the adobe was too wet to work, the Yoshidas kept right on with their plans.

Anna's father died in March. There were days of solemnity, according to the Buddhist rites. It was then that Mrs. Douglass learned that Anna's husband, in marrying her, had consented to assume her family's name, because there was no son in Anna's family, and the name would have perished. That explained why the old Mrs. Yoshida was really Anna's mother, not her mother-in-law.

The first time that Mrs. Douglass' saw old Mrs. Yoshida she almost felt within her hands again the soft, paper-bound copy of a Japanese fairy tale which she had cherished when she was Marion's age, a story about an old woman who lost her rice dumpling and went through strange adventures in her attempt to recover it. The face of old Mrs. Yoshida, brown and soft and encircled with wrinkles, was for all the world like the face of the old woman in the illustrations. Perhaps it was for that Mrs. Douglass felt so fond of the old Mrs. Yoshida. At any rate, without a word of any language in common between them, they got along beautifully.

Mrs. Douglass had the dimmest of ideas about the Buddhist faith. She had read, once upon a time, a little book in French called *Les Paroles du Boudhha,* and had reflected that in the main the Buddha had sounded very Christian. She had a natural Western aversion to the idea of nirvana, and that was doubtless important to the doctrine, but the teaching of pity and kindliness was Christian enough. She had an idea that Buddhists were distinct from Shintoists, and she preferred Buddhists. But even in her state of occidental ignorance she could not overlook nor misunderstand the deep religious feeling of the Yoshida family at the time of their loss.

Old Mrs. Yoshida worked in the fields too. The little boy played at the end of the furrows by the raised edge of the big ditch or dabbled in the wooden irrigating troughs. They were all in the fields the greater part of the day, and the house was silent and deserted.

Then, toward the end of May, Mrs. Douglass heard that Anna had been taken with "very bad pains" as she was working in the berry patch, and, although the doctor was sent for and came as soon as she could, the baby came faster, several months too early, a girl. The doctor wrapped up the little creature, so imperfectly equipped for life outside her mother's body, and took her to the hospital, where the infant was tucked into an incubator and given a mixture of oxygen and carbon dioxide.

The baby lived. When she was returned to Anna, she weighed less than three pounds, but she was healthy. They named her May, for the month in which she was born, and in order that she might have an American name when she should be ready for school. At home they called her Michiko.

Kathryn Douglass had never seen any human being so small or so exquisite. Anna came in from the fields— she had hardly been away from her work for more than three days—and unwrapped the bundle lying on the double bed.

"The hands," said Kathryn Douglass, "they're unbelievable!" And they were, the palm the size of a five-cent piece, the fingers with the perfection of the stamens of a flower.

She brought down later some garments which had been too small for Marion ever to wear, when she was a baby, glad that they were still fresh and untubbed and new-looking, and Anna laid them aside for the baby to grow into. Marion came too, to observe, silent and round-eyed.

They were all glad that the baby throve. Month by month she gained, making up the handicap of her early birth, until the time came when she was introduced to food other than that with which Anna's brown breast had supplied her. Kathryn Douglass was surprised and flattered when Anna came to her, asking advice about infant diet. She brought out the government pamphlet by which Marion's existence had been ruled, and underlined paragraphs for Anna, and read them to her, and then gave her the booklet; and Anna, abandoning the advice of old Mrs. Yoshida, followed the instructions with conscience. Michiko was fed according to the advice of the Children's Bureau, the best American advice. When she was three years old it was hard to remember, or even imagine, how minute she once had been, how fragile, with what precarious hold on life. Brown-skinned and red-lipped, and round of face, she ran about the farmyard and the wide acres in castoff overalls of her brother Isamu. Kathryn Douglass was perhaps to be pardoned for feeling a possessive interest in her. And in the Yoshida family.

Through the years she had come to know the interior of the Yoshida house, the big kitchen upon which all the other rooms, the bedrooms, opened, for there was no living room. In a glass vase in the center of the kitchen table there was always a collection of chopsticks; it was like the glass tumbler full of spoons on an American farmhouse table. She knew the wood stove and the kerosene lamps, the Japanese calendars which were the only adornment of the room, the muddy shoes removed and left by the back door, the summer kitchen, windowless and cool, with big stone crocks; and, in the yard, the small bathhouse, the packing shed at the edge of the fields. She always entered the house with hesitancy, in fear of intrusion, and was always greeted with the greatest deference. It was always like entering into someplace foreign, and yet it was familiar, being so bare, so reduced to the first elements of housekeeping.

Gifts from the Yoshida fields entered the Douglass kitchen, the freshest lettuce, the biggest and greenest bunches of celery, boxes of strawberries or raspberries, and salad greens for which there were no English names and for which Mrs. Douglass never could learn the Japanese. Perhaps it was a feathery green thing like carrot tops in appearance, tasting faintly like oxalis, more delicate than chicory; perhaps some other unfamiliar leaf, but always good. Sometimes Mrs. Douglass bought bean curd and soy sauce from Anna, but always under protest, for the Yoshidas did not like to sell her things; they liked to make presents. That was of course very Japanese. But Kathryn Douglass liked to make presents too, and it kept up a pleasant social intercourse, full of small surprises, and—there was no denying it—brightened the days not a little. The Douglass family remembered for a long time a Christmas gift of raspberry wine, red as no grape wine ever was, pellucid and rich and smelling like berry patches in the summer sun.

There was also to be remembered the rainy autumn when Mrs. Douglass had been ill. She had been sick for a week, or longer, and the household was in confusion, when Anna appeared on the doorstep, indignant and wronged.

"You should tell me," she said to Mr. Douglass, "because when Mrs. Douglass is sick I will come and work and not charge you anything."

He had been glad enough to have her there, but when it came time to pay her, and he was unable to force any money into her hand, he was indignant, and scolded his wife. He did not like to be beholden to people who worked so hard, who existed on such a narrow financial margin as the Yoshidas. He could afford to pay and Anna could not afford to work for nothing, he argued, but his argument had no effect upon Anna.

"Just the same," he said, "you shouldn't let her do it."

"*You* talk to her," said his wife.

Looking back upon it, Kathryn Douglass hardly knew how the affection had sprung up, and did not try to overestimate it. The bond was tenuous, but it was there, and it held, even after the Douglasses had left the old place and moved some eight miles inland for the dryer climate. At holiday time the Yoshidas' old car drew up at the new place, or Kathryn Douglass would come home from shopping late some evening to find the porch piled with vegetables enough for a whole neighborhood. Marion accumulated charming and semiuseless Japanese belong-

ings, and time of its own weight endowed small events
with great meaning. Marion was practically grown up,
Billy was going to school, and Kathryn Douglass no
longer had a baby about the house. Sometimes she
thought wistfully of Marion's earliest, staggering prom-
enades; little and curly-headed, with such fat short legs
that her mother sometimes thought she must be knock-
kneed, a two-year-old Marion had a way of escaping from
her mother's distinct recollection. Yet when the small
image did return, colored and clear, to Kathryn
Douglass's eye, often as not the child would be standing
at the edge of the Yoshidas' lettuce patch, or leaning, to
watch with Isamu, the water running in the wooden
irrigating troughs. So that to remember her daughter as a
child was often the same thing as to remember Anna,
Michiko, or Isamu.

And now the Yoshidas were to be exiled, along with
all the other coastal-dwelling Japanese. Kathryn Douglass
had no doubts about the wisdom of the measure. She had
no theories about understanding the Japanese mind. She
had never possessed any. Part of the charm of the
Yoshidas was that she never "understood" them. She was
only fond of them. Yet she did not distrust them per-
sonally. She felt that it would be wise to remove all the
Japanese from the coast, as much to safeguard the loyal
Japanese from the consequences of the treachery of the
disloyal as to protect the coast from the acts of traitors.
She did not doubt that there were traitors; neither did
she doubt that there were very many loyal Japanese.
But she had no theories about how to separate the loyal
from the disloyal. There seemed no way to X-ray a mind
and find out what went on within it.

She did not know just what the Yoshidas thought about the war. Her one interview with Anna since Pearl Harbor had been shortly after Christmas. The Japanese had foreseen that they were to be moved. Anna had asked to be given recommendations for housework. She would not be working in the fields any more. The fields would not be replanted this year.

The Yoshida car stopped beyond the gate. Kathryn Douglass, still standing with her hands upon the morning's summary of tragedy, heard a small commotion of farewells, and then Anna came into the yard with her arms full of packages. She came into the living room, bent over her bundles, smiling and bowing, a small brown woman, bundled into an old brown coat, so that she looked like a wren with her feathers rounded out against the cold. Her hair was sleek and black; her eyes were bright. There was still, on her lower lip, as when Kathryn Douglass had first seen her, a kind of little blister, or scar, like a small grain of rice. She put her bundles down on the table. The paper disappeared from view.

"Anna," said Kathryn Douglass with belated compunction, "I forgot that you were working out this winter. Did I break into one of your regular days?"

"That's all right, Mrs. Douglass," said Anna. "I told the lady I couldn't come today. I make it up to her some other time, maybe Sunday, when she has a party."

"I wouldn't have wanted you to do that," said Mrs. Douglass, wondering guiltily if the other lady were feeling as disconcerted as she herself had felt a short time earlier.

"That's all right, Mrs. Douglass," said Anna. "Don't

you worry about that. I told you so long time ago that when you need me I come." She continued, shyly, "I brought some things. You want to see them now?"

"Of course. What kind of things?"

Anna giggled. "Oh, not much. Just some funny things for the children."

The wrappings began to fall to right and left. Two boxes emerged, of satiny balsa wood. Anna slid back the cover of one and began to lift out little packages wrapped in crumpled tissue paper. A tree, with a gnarled black trunk and brilliant green pine needles, very small. A jointed rod with little pulleys. A black lacquered platform. A black lacquered gate or bit of fence. A little man, frozen in a pose of utmost effort, leaning back and pulling on an invisible rope. A stuffed fish. A rope. Pinwheels of gold and black. Anna smiled at the mystification in the other woman's face. She began to fit the various small things together. She was very intent. She had forgotten just how everything should be, and stood, with the fantastic little pinwheels in her hand, meditating, then seemed to remember, laid them aside, and began with the man and the gate.

The plan began to emerge, and after a few minutes there it was, a scene, mounted on the lacquer platform, of a very proud Japanese father hauling on a rope from which floated, beyond the tip of the tiny lacquered pole, a fish kite, black and gold. The pinwheels stood out from the tip of the pole; the pine tree was part of the background, and the little gate braced the pole. The father, dressed in black and purple, with his forehead blue where the hair had been shaved, and the long hair done up on the top of his head, looked as if he had come straight from an old print. He was tradition personified. The whole scene was altogether charming and exquisite. Anna stood back and admired it.

"There," she said. "For Boy Day. For Billy."

Kathryn Douglass admired it too. She felt something curiously like a lump in her throat as she tried to make the proper remarks of appreciation. No other offering could have brought back so suddenly into the dolorous morning the wide fields in May and the first kites which she had ever been privileged to own. Two mothers of sons, they stood in the disheveled room and admired the little man in all his pride and firmness.

"The other box?" inquired Mrs. Douglass.

"Oh, that one? Not so pretty. For Boy Day, too, but you could give it to the girl." Anna took out a bear and a triumphant fat little boy with flying black locks. These figures, set upon another black lacquered platform, with another little twisted tree, and some other bits of scene setting, became the tableau of an infant hero who had wrestled with a bear and overthrown him. The bear lay at his feet with his paws in the air. It was very amusing. Mrs. Douglass knew that Marion would adore it.

"But, Anna," she said, "these were given to Isamu. Don't you think you ought to keep them?"

Anna shook her head sadly. "No place."

"Then let me keep them for you until you all come back again. We will enjoy them just as much."

"No," said Anna. "Maybe we never come back, not here. Who knows? You take them. I like you to have them."

She gathered up a last package, wrapped in newspaper. She said sadly, "Onions, lettuce. You can use?"

"Of course," said Mrs. Douglass quickly. "Awfully glad to have them. Oh, it *is* too bad that you all have to go away. We are going to miss you."

Anna looked down sadly at the package of onions and lettuce.

"Yes, we miss you too," she said. "I guess it better, though. People don't want us here. We make them feel bad. So we better go." Then she became very practical. "You go now, Mrs. Douglass, you go work. I take care everything. Don't you worry. I go work."

In the security of the back bedroom where she kept her typewriter Mrs. Douglass sat and looked at the last pages of her story. She was not in the least interested in it. Perfunctorily she typed out a few sentences, then sat back and stared at the page.

The little man with the fish kite had looked wonderfully elegant on the piano, and the quintessence of all that was Japanese. How long would she have the courage to leave it there, after today? she wondered. Not that she didn't like it herself, or that her husband would object, or even that she was afraid of being called pro-Japanese by the neighbors, but that Harriet might come in, or some other person who, like Harriet, had felt already the bitterness of the war to its full extent. Thinking of Harriet, she could not admire herself for her own tolerance. Her husband was just a year or so too old for the Army, her boy many years safely too young; she was going to be out of it as far as most personal loss was involved. And yet Harriet was her own cousin, and Harriet's boy —well, he could never have been as close to Billy as she had been to Harriet, but still, it was mostly for that boy that she woke each morning with such a sense of desolation. There was still a chance that he might come through, of course, but how slim a chance she did not like to think.

She reread the sentences she had written and found them very dull. She tried to recast the thought in sprightlier language and the effort made her feel slightly nauseated—drained, empty, and ill. The whole business of writing stories in such times seemed so useless. Yet people did need something to read besides the newspapers, something not too far above their daily lives. Even Harriet. She would do anything for Harriet, even write nonsense. Then her cousin's drawn face crowded between her and the typewritten page.

"It is silly, Katy, to try to underestimate the danger. I might just as well begin facing it now as later. If we get him back, God knows that will be wonderful . . . if he doesn't have to suffer too much before we get him back. You don't think the Japanese love us any more than they do the Chinese? I think they hate us worse—they've been saving it up for so long. And you know what you told me about your friend, that girl who came in from Shanghai on the *President Hoover?* Remember?"

Kathryn Douglass remembered; she had told it all to Harriet. That was before there had seemed to be any danger of Harriet's having to be concerned with such terrors herself. She wished that Harriet would not remember. But Harriet insisted.

"Remember, you told me how she came out to see you, after the boat docked? She was so brave, so self-contained, so calm about having been through a bombing—several bombings—you thought she was a miracle. You gave her the best lunch you could cook—fresh strawberry shortcake, and all that, and she was so gracious to the people you had invited to meet her. I know—they were people she had asked to see—you weren't putting her on exhibition. And you sat and marveled at her all through luncheon. Remember? And then that awful gastritis, that had her all but screaming, and she thought it was cholera, because she'd been working with the coolies before she left?"

"Of course I remember, Hattie, but don't let's talk about it now."

"Why not?" said Harriet. "It tells me something I have to know. Corregidor isn't going to hold out forever. She was a nurse, but still she was too sick to tell you what to do for her. So you phoned the doctor. And you gave her that salt-and-sugar enema. And she began to vomit. And when it was all over and you had her tucked in bed, she began to talk. And that was just like the vomiting and the enema all over again, except that she poured it out of her memory, all the horror, the mutilations she had seen, the Chinese babies gathered up from the streets, some alive, and some not."

"Don't, Hattie, for the love of goodness, don't remember."

"But I have to," said Harriet. "For an hour she lay there and told you all those things that you told me, all those things that she had either seen herself or heard from Chinese or from other missionary nurses—and not just for Shanghai but for all China. They all knew it, those people, knew what was happening to China and what was going to happen to us, and we didn't really listen to them; not as we should have. So now I have to remember, because I don't want to go on in a daydream through the rest of this war."

Kathryn Douglass laid her arms across her typewriter and bowed her head on them and felt almost as sick as her friend had felt. And in all her misery, suddenly she was seeing a dark evening on the road to the old place, figures gathered on the muddy ground before the Yoshidas' house, figures surrounding Anna, who stood with Isamu clasped to her breast, a small Isamu, three years old, and through the dim air she could see Anna's face, and the anguish with which she held the little boy so close to her.

"The horse kicked him," said Anna, whispering, "kicked his head."

All the other figures about Anna were helpless with anxiety, and the air itself was filled with their concern, their tenderness, their pity. Well, Isamu had not died. The white scar was under his thick, soft black hair. It was all right. At least, that was all right.

With a sigh she lifted her head from her arms, straightened the pages of the manuscript which lay beside the machine, and slowly got back to work. After all, Anna had given her this morning for a purpose, and besides, there was a deadline to meet. It meant something to the Douglass finances.

About twelve-thirty she pulled the last sheet from the typewriter, clipped the story together, put the cover on the machine, and went in search of Anna. She found her on her knees, putting a luster on the living-room floor with a piece of lambskin cut from a long-discarded bedroom slipper. The room was immaculate. There were flowers on the mantel, more sprays of her yellow jasmine, and the brass andirons shone like gold; the greenery through the windows was as fresh as after a rain because the windows had been polished. The little man still balanced his weight against the pull of the fish kite on the piano. The room had never been more charming. Leaning against the doorjamb, because her knees seemed to be shaking, Kathryn Douglass considered that it would not matter that evening whether the hostess were entertaining or not. The room itself would be sufficient hospitality.

Anna looked up at her, smiling.

"I getting along fine," she said. "You have good morning?"

"Awful morning," said Mrs. Douglass, realizing that her head ached and that she felt totally exhausted.

Anna's face looked suddenly disconsolate.

"But I finished the story," Mrs. Douglass hastened to explain. "I can copy the rest of it this afternoon and mail it in the morning. It's all right. I just feel tired."

"Oh," said Anna. "I get you quick some lunch. I proud you finish the story. I make you quick some tea."

They went into the kitchen together. As she brought out eggs and butter, laid places for two on the kitchen table, Mrs. Douglass felt that she was indeed very tired. She had returned to Anna after a vague but terrifying experience, and she felt a great desire to protect Anna from that experience. She must be careful about what she said to Anna. She sat down at the table, resting her head on her hands while Anna scrambled the eggs and made the tea. When Anna slipped into the chair across from her she could not help taking comfort from the sight of her soft brown face. Very proud, very unassuming was Anna Yoshida. It sounded like an impossible combination, but there it was. Very remote, belonging to a foreign way of life, and yet affectionate, near, familiar. Of what age was Anna? Mrs. Douglass wondered. With a skin like that, so easily wrinkled and so often exposed to the elements, it was hard to decipher the years. And the other clues to a woman's age, the way she wore her hair, or liked to dress, were entirely missing. Anna's hair was brushed back smoothly from her round forehead and pinned in a knot at the back of her neck. Her clothes were any garments which would keep her warm.

"Where were you born, Anna?" asked Kathryn Douglass.

"In Japan," said Anna.

"But when did you come to this country?"

"Oh, long ago. I was a little girl."

"But you did not grow up like the Nisei."

"No, I grow up old style."

The onions were very crisp and delicate, the tea fragrant and hot. As she sipped the tea her eyes met those of Anna above the cup, and Anna's eyes were reassuring. Mrs. Douglass began to feel less tired. Either it was the effect of the tea, or of something harder to describe.

"How is Michiko?" she asked.

"Oh, she's *fat*," said Anna, laughing.

They talked about the children, Isamu, Marion, Billy. "I never finished to pay the doctor yet," said Anna. "I always want to. But the celery this year—everybody have such good crops, we have almost to give it away."

"The doctor? For what?" said Mrs. Douglass.

"Why, for Michiko."

"Michiko? After all these years?"

"Yes—that very bad, after all these years. I still want to."

Kathryn Douglass nibbled at an onion, smaller than a pencil, crisp as snow, and thought of all the sweet crisp celery, all the big green heads of lettuce, all the fragrant berries the Yoshidas had coaxed from the Dutchman's fields since she had first known them. She thought also of how little they had asked in return, or had received, besides the privilege of living unmolested on those wide acres in sight of the mountains and in sight of the bay. She wondered if they had ever bought any new clothes. But Isamu and Michiko could go to school, walking along the dike by the big ditch across lots to the schoolhouse. It was a nice school. Kathryn Douglass knew most of the children there. They were the Manchesters, the Kellys, the Cardozas, the Combatalades, the Ferrantis, the Perraults, the Mocks, the Yoshidas. It sounded like an international settlement, but it wasn't. It was only a nice country school. On the other hand, it was heaven.

"Michiko fat," she said dreamily. "Imagine. Do you remember when all the things I brought her were always too big for her? Anna, did you get your license for the car again?"

"Yes'm," said Anna. "We had lot of trouble with it, but I do what you say. I send white slip to Tadashi and he sign it. So it all right."

Tadashi was Anna's nephew. He was a Nisei, and the car was in his name.

"Where is Tadashi?" asked Kathryn Douglass, off her guard.

"He in the Army," said Anna.

So here it was again, the war. They had almost lost

it. For a while two women, fond of each other, interested in each other's children, they had almost put it out of existence. But there it was again. And again she felt very tired. She said wearily:

"That was a nice lunch, Anna. Now I'd better go copy that story."

"You tell me," said Anna, "what you want for supper, I get things ready. I fix vegetables and set table. So you lie down and rest little bit before those people come."

"You spoil me, Anna," said Mrs. Douglass.

"I don't p'raps have much other chance to spoil you ever again may be," said Anna.

They had been so careful. They had hardly mentioned Anna's going away. But that was foolish.

"Anna," said Mrs. Douglass, and felt her throat tighten in spite of herself, "you must write to me, you know, and tell me what you need, and what I can get for you. I will always be so glad to do anything I can. You will remember that, won't you?"

"Yes'm," said Anna. "I write. I promise."

Kathryn Douglass could see the tears in the eyes of Anna Yoshida, very bright tears in the corners of very bright, almond-shaped eyes. She blinked hard. There were tears in her own eyes.

"You go work now," said Anna Yoshida. "Let me get busy. This kitchen, it so dirty, Mrs. Douglass, I ashamed for you."

Picnic, 1943

THEY ARRIVED at the white iron gates without getting lost on the way, although there was one confusing moment when University Avenue turned out to be an unpaved lane, overhung by wild lilac and lustrous branches of poison oak. The two boys were waiting for them at the gates, as promised, Dmitri on the right- and Brian on the left-hand post, both with their bare brown knees tucked up under their chins, and the foliage—fortunately not poison oak this time—crowding behind them as they looked down from the green shadows. The posts were square, with architectural panelings on the side, and wide flat tops. She could tell, after one glance at them, that the house would be in the most formidable style of the 1890s, and probably painted white to match the gate.

Dmitri descended like a lizard, brown, slender, and quick, and came to stand on the running board, hooking his bare arm through the window on the right. Brian, descending more slowly, took a slow and candid look at the guests and then disappeared up the curving road.

"Straight ahead," said Dmitri. "What are we waiting for?"

"I'm afraid I'll brush you off," she said.

"Not me," said Dmitri. "My mother is waiting for you at the house. Then we go down to the stream." He peered under the roof of the car, a pointed brown face with impish flaring eyebrows above tawny golden eyes, very alert and inquiring. "You wore your old clothes? That's fine. It's not at all clean at the stream. Mud, you know. The last people who came for a picnic, they looked so beautiful, but we didn't have any fun. Too clean."

The car lurched heavily to the side as the road took on the character of a stream bed, and the brown hand tightened its hold, the small arm grew tense, but the smile remained undisturbed. When the road forked, Dmitri indicated the correct turn. They went mostly uphill, turning and twisting, and once the children in the back seat let out a cry of "The creek! The creek!" as a gleam of water showed through the tangled dark foliage on the lower side of the road. Then suddenly they emerged upon a formal graveled space, surrounded by neglected but nevertheless formal flower beds.

"To the right," said Dmitri, and there the car stopped directly in front of the steps to the veranda.

Meredith Jones got out of the car and stretched her legs. Then she tipped up the driver's seat and let the children crawl out, a little boy of five, a girl of six, an older girl; all three of them disappeared around the end of the car to join Dmitri. Brian was already there. He had beat the car to the house.

Ted Nash let himself out, stretched his long frame, and then slumped, with his hands in his pockets.

"Picnics," he said with a sigh. "Oh well, it's good for the children, I presume."

"I only hope it's a good picnic," said Mrs. Jones. "It's a long way to come with gas what it is."

"More precious than liquor," said Nash. "At picnics we drink milk, don't we?"

"Do you like milk, Ted?" inquired Molly Leontovich. She had come out on the porch and stood there, smiling at them, a ruffled dimity apron tied on over her denim slacks, her lovely red hair and lovely Irish smile shining upon them.

Nash didn't answer. He jammed his hands deeper in his pockets and tipped his head back to look at her from under his eyelids, in the manner of the nearsighted.

Molly said, "There's some corn liquor in the kitchen. You ought to see my kitchen. It's terrific. Besides, you could peel potatoes for me."

Mrs. Jones had the impression, just before they entered the house, of more bay windows than she had ever before seen affixed to one dwelling. Within, the impression was reinforced by bay windows which enlarged each room by at least one third of its original rectangle. Doubtless a cottage in the mind of its architect, for it was only one story high, the house had yet been endowed with all possible grandeur in the way of high ceilings, deep windows, and marble fireplaces, and in all this architectural grandeur with discolored paint and faded wallpaper stood the oddest and scantiest collection of secondhand furniture that Meredith Jones had ever yet laid eyes on.

"This," said Molly, waving her hands at the discredited walls and woodwork, "is going to be beautiful.

I'm going to paint it pale green with cream-colored wood-work, and have the walls frescoed with magnolia blossoms, and always keep a fresh magnolia in a green glass vase on a low table in the alcove there by the windows. Won't it be lovely?"

She looked at Mrs. Jones as if it were all there ready and visible to be admired. Meredith Jones stretched her imagination and admired it.

"And this is the horrific kitchen," said Molly. "Enter and be at home."

Ted Nash and Meredith Jones followed her into a room which barely held the three of them, the coal stove, the wooden sink, the necessary cupboards, and a table. Here the architect had lost all interest in his project. It was the kitchen for a hovel. But through the window, which was indeed large for the room, Meredith glimpsed the neglected formal garden, and, beyond it, the wall of verdure. She glimpsed also a beautiful roan mare which was wandering about the place with all the freedom of a pet dog.

"Your horse is loose," she said.

"That's Anna Karenina," said Molly, "and she wanders around like that all the time. We haven't been able to fence a paddock yet. After all, we've only been here a month."

Meredith Jones pressed closer to the window. The children had entered the picture now, and she was watching Anna drop her beautiful head affectionately over Dmitri's shoulder. Dmitri put up an arm to embrace her and went on with his harangue to the children, his other arm gesturing widely. Behind Meredith, Ted Nash was explaining:

"My wife works, the husband of Mrs. Jones works, we are the only members of the leisure class in our families —although I do labor on other days than Saturdays—and we have decamped with the only means of transportation in our two families; therefore you need not be concerned about any respective wife or husband dropping in on you at the last minute and asking for food. In fact, we are on the loose. But why such an immense number of boiled potatoes? I thought this was a picnic for the children. In fact," he continued in his gently insulting manner, "I only came in order to bring my child."

"Yes, yes," said Molly reflectively, without being insulted, "that's the way it started, but then Anton invited a few neighbors—I don't know just who or how many." She poured a couple of drinks in an absent-minded fashion, put down the bottle, and began to rummage in a box of knives and spoons. "I can't find anything here," she complained. "Besides, we left all the good and useful things at the house when we rented it. It's incredible how much money you can get for renting a house that's furnished down to toothpicks and nutcrackers. It's incredible too how hard it is to find a decent paring knife these days." She came upon a small knife with a red composition handle and presented it to Nash. "Drink your liquor," she said, "and then start in on those potatoes. And be careful of the knife. I had another one like it, but I broke it cutting butter. The handle broke in my hand."

Meredith said, "No drink for me."

"All right then," said Molly. "Your friend can have two."

The phone rang, and she went off to answer it. Ted

Nash drank his liquor and said that it wasn't bad. He gave Meredith a chance to change her mind about the other glass. She shook her head. He helped himself to it.

"You don't explain much about these picnics you bring me on," he complained. "Who are these people?"

"You met them," she said. "At the Hendershots'."

"Yes, I know," he said. "You said they were White Russians. They came very late. But Molly—that hair."

"Molly's from south of the slot," said Meredith patiently. "Her name was Coyle. And Anton was the Czar's something or other. Not an admiral. Something on horseback. And he's very distinguished."

"I admit it," said Nash. "And now he's working in a defense plant. With the admiral. There is an admiral in the defense plant, isn't there?"

"I think so," said Meredith. She hunted out another knife and began to peel potatoes. Ted Nash began to peel potatoes also. Molly Leontovich returned from her phone call.

"That was my little stepdaughter," she said. "She's coming to supper and wants to bring some friends. I don't believe there are enough potatoes, do you? I'd better cook some more."

"How many friends?" asked Nash. "There are a lot of potatoes here right now."

Molly said, "Four or five. Ed Stebbins and his family, and someone else, some other Party member."

"Ed Stebbins!" said Nash, overcome with wonder. "And I thought you were White Russians."

Molly took her attention from the potatoes long enough to be amused at him. "Sonya is very Red," she informed him. "Very, very Red. And Ed Stebbins is very entertaining. A wonderful man."

"But what does your husband think of all this?"

"Oh, it's all right. These are Reds, not Russians. Except Sonya. And anyway, the White Russians are all so pleased now with the Bolshies. They brag about them. After all, they are Russians too, and they have been magnificent.

"And as for Sonya, you can't blame her. She's young, and she remembers being so hungry in Russia. Her mother died of malnutrition—starvation, you know—although they called it something else. And she has little pocks in the enamel of her teeth because she never got enough milk when she was a kid. The lipstick always rubs off on the edges of them. Not that it hurts her looks. She's so pretty—just wait till you see her. And so . . ."

"So what?"

"So she feels she wants to do something about it—you know, about Russian kids not getting enough milk."

"But what about your husband?" inquired Nash, determined to get to the bottom of the matter. "Is he still White?"

Molly made an impatient gesture.

"He was always White. It's like being born a Southerner. But he doesn't mind about Sonya. After all, he's an intelligent man." She suddenly remembered about the children. "Where have they gone?" she asked Meredith.

"They're with Dmitri."

Molly appeared worried. "I should go after them; I don't like such little ones down at the creek alone. Dmitri has sense—but not all the time, and the pools are still very deep. I think I'll go and see what they're up to."

"I'll go," said Meredith.

"Would you, darling?" said Molly. "I meant to have everything ready before you came, so that we could all go down together." She went to the porch with Meredith and pointed out the path to the creek. "We'll be down as soon as we get the salad made. We'll bring everything. You're an angel. And I am so glad you brought Mr. Nash. I need a man to help carry things—Anton gets home so late."

So Meredith Jones went down to the creek. The woods were very quiet and hot. The air, too dry to be sultry, seemed close, nevertheless, because it was unmoving. During the drive down the valley, on their way to the Leontovich place, she had noticed how the hills were veiled in haze that was like the day's heat made visible. It had been a hot day and she was tired, and glad to be by herself for a few minutes.

In California the creeks run full in the spring and dwindle through the summer months to a few pools or a few damp places in the sand. All the torrent-tossed rubble of the winter is left in the gullies. The secret conformations of the stream bed are exposed to the sunlight, and the children stand on the dry bottoms and look up to the high-water marks and remember or imagine how violent and fresh and lavish the stream was the winter before. The stream which the Leontovich family called theirs was better than most. Now, in early July, it still had some deep pools, as Molly had said, some shallows where the water ran with an audible ripple, and also some rocky islands and shoals, suitable for picnics, if you were not fussy about sitting upon rocks or upon the grassless earth. In the woods at this season there was poison oak, and in the fields there were foxtails, a diabolical kind of little dry, wheatlike sticker, so that, taking it all in all, a stream bed was by far the nicest place for a picnic.

When Meredith Jones reached the edge of the gully she heard joyous cries and splashing noises, and she arrived, sliding and running down the steep bank side, at the stony floor of the creek just in time to see Sally Nash totter and sit down in the shallow water.

Her own son and Dmitri roared with laughter. Sally, after the first gasp, shrieked with triumph also. Brian, solid and serious, stood on the graveled sandspit and urged Sally to get up because she was getting all wet. Meredith looked about for her daughter, who was no-where to be seen.

There was nothing to be done about Sally for the present. The late afternoon was still so warm that there was no danger of her catching cold. When the sun went, and the chill began to descend, they would just have to borrow something of Brian's from Molly to wrap the child up in. Brian looked more of a size with Sally than did Dmitri. Meredith Jones sat down on a rock beside the shallows and smiled at Sally. After all, what good was a brook if you couldn't get wet in it?

It was nice here. It was a long way out of the world. Meredith Jones sat and observed how the water lights re-flected upward into Sally's face, and how the leaf shadows from above made her pale hair look greenish. The hair of her own son, under the same light, looked a darker brown, more nearly a chestnut than it really was, as the round head bent toward the water. Something atavistic possessed the children. Water, the aboriginal playmate, had filled them all with an excitement that was not hysterical but an abandonment, and a release. Young Jones suddenly lifted his head and looked about him with a radiant face. He ignored his mother, although he must have seen her, and after a long joyous look all about the scene, wheeled and plowed slowly downstream through the water past Sally to a narrow beach. Dmitri dashed by him, leaped to the steep bank, swung up and around a buttress of roots which the spring flood had washed bare, and curved down again and into the water.

Meredith Jones clasped her hands about her knees and leaned back to look up at the sky. The banks rose on either hand more than twice the height of her standing figure, clothed with young bay trees, bushlike, that had resisted the water, and crowned at the level of the woods with great bay trees that must have been growing there for years and years. The plumed tops swept upward, lifting the gully walls higher and higher, and leaving only a winding strip of sky that followed the journeyings of the creek. Upstream and downstream the gully turned abruptly, barring the vision. It was a wonderfully secluded and remote spot.

After a while Meredith's eleven-year-old daughter Marylin appeared, with her hands full of trophies—flowers, ferns, a spray of eucalyptus pods. She arranged a pool at the edge of the sand bar for a vase where she anchored her flowers, and then rolled up her jeans and joined the smaller children in the water. Time went by, and Meredith Jones lost all track of the passing of it. She did not know whether they had been there a long time or a short time, when Sally came dripping from the stream to complain that she was hungry. It had been so nice to sit there without responsibility, forgetting the defense plants and everything connected with them, and watch the children being happy.

Dmitri materialized behind Sally, the tawny, almost wholly naked figure akin to the rocks and water and leaf shadows, and explained, half scoffing and half consoling, that meals were always late at his house but that they always appeared in the end.

"It will be good, too, when it gets here," he said, rubbing his bare stomach and grinning.

The light, hitting sideways upon the crests of the trees, did indicate that it was past the children's usual suppertime. Meredith Jones surveyed the wet form of Sally Nash, to which the dripping garments clung like draperies in ancient Greek sculptures, and suggested that Dmitri run up to the house on a double errand: dry clothes for Sally and some information about the progress of the potato salad. He was about to leave when the soft flutter and roar of the blimp's propellers was heard, growing steadily louder and nearer, echoing down into their retreat, and he had to stay, of course, to see it go by overhead.

"How low!" he said joyfully. "She's almost brushing the treetops. You can see all the wires, and the flag!"

Indeed the blimp was very low, heading upstream almost as if following the wooded line of the creek. For a minute it was there, plain to behold, all silver and smooth, and then it crossed the line of trees at the bend and was immediately lost to them.

"So low!" Dmitri exulted. "Do you think they saw us? I waved." Then he was gone.

Marylin, dropping down beside her mother, remarked, "That was the 118. Bob Gaby's ship. He came over school one day when we were having P.E. and dropped apples down."

Her mother expressed her astonishment.

"Yeh," said Marylin. "He's one of Mrs. Cook's old boys. Whenever he's over the school he tries to wiggle his wings at her, or whatever it is you do with a blimp. I got one of the apples."

It seemed pleasant to Meredith Jones that a friend of the children's was aloft overhead, patrolling the mountains and the coast, pleasant and safe. She smiled at the idea of apples dropping on the playground. Of course the coast had been in no danger from the Japs now for months and months, even if there were still Japs on Kiska. The real feeling of uneasiness had all died away at the end of the first summer. The wardens, it was true, had been getting some good if belated training. She had been hearing about it from their next-door neighbor, Jim Sweitzer. It did seem belated, to a mere civilian like herself. That was, she supposed, all a part of getting things nicely in order at last. The blimps, so frequent in that area of the coast, made everything seem very safe. She stretched herself and turned to see what had become of her son. The passing of the blimp had been the only landmark in time since she had left the highway that afternoon.

Dmitri was back soon, laden with dry garments and with pillows which his mother had sent to mitigate the hardness of the rocks. He came down the steep bank in three leaps and dumped everything beside Mrs. Jones. He was followed almost immediately by Ted Nash and a young woman, and another girl of about Marylin's age, both of them strangers to Meredith. Ted did not bother to introduce the young woman; he had probably forgotten her name. He brought the news that the salad was progressing nicely, and busied himself with disrobing his daughter. He seated himself near Meredith and, drawing Sally close to him, attempted to rub her dry with his handkerchief. The young woman sat down on the other side of Meredith, smiling shyly but without embarrassment, apparently willing to take Mrs. Jones on faith. Dmitri, selecting a few of the softer pillows, encamped himself by the newcomer, for once in a mood of domestication. Ted clothed his daughter, bit by bit, and young Jones forsook the stream for his mother's side.

They were all there, gathered closely into a group, as if the increasing lateness of the afternoon drew them together in a sort of home-coming gesture. Meredith heard a plane approaching from downstream, the concentrated sound so much firmer and louder, by virtue of being concentrated, than the loose roar of the blimp, and leaned back to watch it pass. The light was on the very tops of the trees now, and when the plane appeared and passed over them, almost directly above them, but not quite—a little to the left—the light actually seemed to flash upon the underside of the wings. It passed above them, just above the treetops, and disappeared completely at the turn of the gully, just as the blimp had done. But as the light had flashed on the underside of the wing, Meredith Jones saw perfectly plainly what she didn't believe she saw.

"Well, for gosh sakes!" she cried.

"Huh?" said Ted Nash, not looking up from a fastening on Sally's overalls.

"Did you see that?" said Meredith.

"What?" said Nash.

"The insignia on that plane. Do we have any planes with big round oranges under the wings?"

"Do you know what oranges under the wings mean?" said Nash sardonically.

"Jap insignia," said Marylin innocently.

"Did you see it, Marylin?" her mother asked eagerly.

"Nope," said Marylin without excitement.

"But, Ted," said Meredith Jones, "I did see it—Jap insignia. Just like those silly women at Pearl Harbor."

"What women?" said Ted, achieving the fastening and turning Sally about for inspection.

"Oh, you know, the ones that ran out shouting, 'It's all right, those planes are from California, they've oranges on their wings.'"

Ted looked at her compassionately. "My dear Meredith," he said in his best professorial manner, "your eyes need examining. There is a little red dot in the middle of a white star."

"I know all about that," said Meredith Jones with impatience. "There wasn't any star. And it wasn't a dot. It was a big round orange."

Ted Nash turned to the young woman beside Meredith and said gently, with a motion of his head toward his friend, "Touched in the head. Sunstroke."

Meredith began to laugh, but she was embarrassed. "It sounds crazy all right, especially just after the blimp. But I did see it."

Dmitri said something then, and the young woman turned to catch it. She made him repeat it.

"What does he say?" inquired Nash.

"He says he saw it. It had big red tomatoes on the wings."

Meredith said nothing. She could not really believe that she had seen a Jap plane. She looked to Nash for an explanation.

"By me," said Nash. "Maybe the Army is sending out some fakes to test out the observers." It was a silly explanation, but it seemed to end the discussion. Dmitri, who was not at all interested, having made his contribution toward the evidence in the case, found one of those strange smooth yellow creatures known to the children as banana slugs, and was showing it to Marylin. Marylin went into shivers of horror and loathing. Dmitri, delighted at the effect of his find, immediately went in search of other slugs, and Marylin followed him, fascinated and loathing. Up the creek they went, with the cries, "Banana slugs! Banana slugs!" ringing in the air, mingled with Marylin's exclamations of disgust.

Molly appeared at the top of the bank with a crowd of people, and baskets. Supper had arrived, and the Japanese plane, or whatever it was, could not compete in interest either with the banana slugs or with the potato salad.

People whom Meredith had never met surrounded her, all acting as if they had known her always. She recognized Anton Leontovich and greeted him. Sonya, as pretty as they come, was handing about paper plates and napkins. She helped Meredith to get the smaller children settled and supplied. The confusion was magnificent, and the creek bottom seemed as populous as the Grand Central Station. In the midst of it all Meredith Jones did ask herself, "What was it I saw if it wasn't a Japanese plane? There's nothing the matter with·my eyes, that I know of, and there's certainly nothing the matter with Dmitri's." Once she asked the young woman what she thought the plane could have been. The young woman smiled rather pityingly, shrugged her shoulders, and said, "I didn't see it." That was the end of it. Nobody wanted to talk about it. Nobody was interested. Nash was engaged in conversation with the great Ed Stebbins. Meredith took her plate of food to a spot near the children and ate her supper tranquilly. She forgot about the Japanese plane. It had no reality, anyway.

Good-bye, Son

~~~~~~

SARA MCDERMOTT stood on the station platform, saying good-bye to her husband. A woman in her early forties, dark-haired and dark-eyed, with a practical, humorous face, bareheaded in the mild December evening, she stood with her hands pushed into the pockets of her gray tweed suit, looking up to Tom Mc-Dermott, where he waited on the platform of the car. Shreds of steam blew past her ankles, and strangers jostled her slightly. Tom smiled at her reservedly, aware of the presence of other people. Bareheaded also, but with his hat in his hand, his heavy overcoat unbuttoned, he shifted his weight from one foot to the other, and said, for the second time: "You won't forget about those papers, Sary? If you can get them in the airmail tomorrow, they'll reach us Monday morning, and goodness knows we're going to need them. I wish I could have finished them up."

"I won't forget," she promised. "I'll have a go at them tonight. And don't you lose those woolen gloves. It's going to be cold in Seattle."

She thought with pride and affection how little the gray showed in his blond hair, and how little apparent, all in all, were his forty-five years. The ruddy face was lined, but no more than was becoming, and the wide-set blue eyes were as clear as ever. The squareness of the face, and the shortness of the nose, which was blunt without being heavy, had something to do with the impression of youthfulness. They looked direct and candid —as he was, as he had always been. The moments of farewell were difficult, because they had nothing more to say, but she was too fond of him to relinquish him before she had to. She kept her eyes fixed on him till the porter closed the doors, then gave him one more quick nod and smile, and turned away before the train pulled out of the station. Looking at people through the windows of a train was too much like looking at them through the glass lid of an old-fashioned coffin. She had had to do that once for an old neighbor at a country burial, and she had done so bravely enough, but she did not relish such things.

She walked briskly to her car and left the station ahead of most of the departing traffic. At the highway she had to stop because of the red light, and as she took her eyes from the road she saw the soldier, standing in the shadow of the hedge, a figure somewhat indistinct because of the color of his uniform against the leaves. He looked toward her, not, it is true, with his thumb in the air, but hopefully, and she thought afterward that she could not have missed him, even if the light had been green. She opened the car door, beckoning to him, and just as the light was about to change, he slid into the seat beside her. She had a quick impression of someone

young and blond, in an outdoors sort of way, and firmly
built, and then it became necessary for her to keep her
eyes on the traffic.

"Awfully nice of you to pick me up," he said as they
moved with the other cars down the highway. The rush
of motors past the opened window blurred his voice
like the sound of water running over it, but even so she
was surprised that it should sound so much like Tom's.
A Middle Western voice it was, and younger than Tom's,
but still very like.

"How far are you going?" she asked, wondering if he
were quartered at the new camp at the edge of town.

"To Carmel," he answered. "I have friends at a place
near there, place called the Highlands."

"Nice place," she said. "I have friends there too."

The voice, heard more distinctly, was perhaps not
quite so much like Tom's, but it was an extremely pleasant voice, and she felt a quick liking for this stranger,
although she had hardly had a chance to look at him.
With that quick liking came an odd feeling of having
experienced something like this before.

She was a conscientious driver, and the traffic was
heavy. It was not until the next stop light that she was
able to turn and look at him properly. The eyes which
met her scrutiny were quite as dark as her own, steady,
and a little amused, perhaps at her direct inspection of
his face. The dark eyes were unusual certainly in a
countenance otherwise so blond—sun- and wind-burned,
ruddy, not tanned; and the close-cropped hair under the
small cap was fair. The shape of the face was squarish,
the nose short and blunt without being heavy. It was
Tom's face, exactly, with her eyes.

"And yet," she thought, "it isn't a duplicate of Tom's at all. It's another person. This is how John would have looked, had he lived to be twenty-one."

She was not entirely unprepared for the resemblance. The voice had startled her, pleasantly but very deeply, and it was as if she had felt, ever since hearing it, that he would look like this. Just the same, she was startled. She thought, rapidly, "This is the way a piano must feel when somebody truly a musician sits down and with both hands strikes hard a finely constructed chord, a chord that has something familiar and satisfying in it, and something new." She did not take time out to think this, but her eyes, glancing over him quickly, noted also the silver bar on his shoulder and the small gold wings on his collar.

"A flier, eh?" she said with a quick smile.

"Yes'm. Bomber pilot."

"And proud of it," she said.

"Yes'm. I only got my bars a few days ago."

"Well, why not?" she said. "Be proud, I mean. You've every right."

How proud she would have been of John! She put the car into gear, as the traffic began to move again, and the soldier answered, in that young voice of Tom's, "I always meant to design planes. But when the defense program started, I thought it might be more fun to fly 'em."

"You'll be a better designer when you get around to it," said Sara McDermott, "than if you hadn't been a flier too."

The soldier made no reply to this, and at the time she did not think of anything sinister in connection with his silence. Although he was quiet, he seemed very alert

and contented. That was one of the first things that im-
pressed her about him, besides the extraordinary resemblance. There was about him a sort of eager serenity,
as if he had all his major decisions safely made and were
only concerned with the extreme interest of being alive.

She said, "My husband designs ships—marine architect, you know."

He merely nodded, without seeming the less friendly,
and she continued, "He started out designing cabin
cruisers in Detroit, years ago. Now he's on his way to
Seattle. I just left him at the station."

"I guess they can use him up there," said the soldier
in cheerful understatement.

She wished he would go on talking, but even when he
didn't it was pleasant having him sitting there beside her.
They had left the town now and were moving along in
full view of the hills, which swept upward, mantled with
the new green of winter, to the watery blue of the
mountains. Above them the clouds were still bright with
sun, although the afternoon was nearly over. After a
while he did begin to talk again, and upon a subject no
less impersonal than the weather.

"I don't get used to California weather," he said. "Look
at today—here it's the sixth of December, and you'd think
it was a day in April, back in Illinois—mighty nice April
day for Illinois, too. Or it might be late fall—Indian
summer. I'm from Illinois, in case you hadn't guessed."

"It might have been Indiana," she answered, "or
Wisconsin, or Michigan."

"Oh, Michigan," he said, "that's the best state in the
union, for me. The northern peninsula. But don't get me
wrong. I like it out here." He went on to speak casually

of the strangeness for him of spring flowers that appeared before the autumn leaves were all off the trees, and, again, of the new grass springing up everywhere now, in December. "Why, even what we'd call a green Christmas in Illinois wasn't green, like this. It was all withered and brown."

Sara McDermott listened to him with deep joy, and, long before they reached the road upon which she usually turned from the highway as she drove home, she knew that she wouldn't have the courage to leave him by the roadside to pick up another ride. That is, she couldn't bear to leave him upon such short acquaintance. Her mind kept going back to John, as was most natural with this living counterpart of John sitting there beside her. John had been born in 1920, and this was 1941.

She said to the soldier, "You're twenty-one, aren't you?"

"That's right," he answered.

"Please don't mind the personal question," she said. "You're something like a boy I used to know. There, do you see that road to the right? That's my road home. We have a little rancho up toward the hills."

"It must be nice," he said politely. "But look here, you shouldn't go out of your way on my account."

"Oh, I'm not," she said. "I've an errand on the highway toward San Jose, and I might just as well do it now as later."

It was perfectly true about the errand, she reflected. She had meant to buy those ranunculus bulbs this week end, but of course she had meant to get them tomorrow, after Tom's papers were safely in the mail. She had seen the sign at the Japanese nursery, twenty-five cents a

dozen, and had thought at once how a dozen or so of
them were needed at the edge of the terrace. But there
was no use in confessing such details to the soldier, not
any more than there would have been in breaking down
and telling him about John. It was enough for her that
he should sit there looking like John, and go on talking
in John's voice about things that John might have remembered. For he had begun to talk about camping trips
in the north woods, about one Christmas vacation when
his father had taken him camping near Marquette, snow
and all. It had been magnificent. And as he talked Sara
McDermott reflected that it was extraordinary that the
resemblance should be more than physical, for this boy
remembered things that John might have remembered,
had he lived. But John had had no life at all. He had
died the same hour he was born. She hadn't even held
him in her arms once, to hear him breathe or feel his
warmth. She was not the person to brood over her loss,
neither when it was new, nor any time afterward, and
now· she drew her thought away from it deliberately.

The countryside, at peace in the departing sunlight,
touched everywhere with that new green which the first
rains had brought, with lines of darker green in the
patches of kale and broccoli, the thickets of pole beans,
lay in a seasonal quiet, a landscape tended but not deserted, for a little time left to itself. Even the vegetable
patches were uninhabited because it was Saturday night.
Far off toward the hills an apricot orchard held a cloud
of dim gold above the green, and there were lines of
russet, close to the earth, where the tenacious bines of
berry bushes held to their leaves. Saturday, with a Sab-
bath quiet already begun, and evening, at the hour when

the light was changing—the familiar landscape, so ample and rich, so deeply at peace, moved her as it had moved her many times before, but never more profoundly. It widened, it seemed, as they advanced, the mountains on the right rising higher, the shapes of mountains toward the east grown more apparent, and, where the orchards parted now and again, beyond the haze of gray prune branches, the silver mound of the great hangar at the air base.

"It's beautiful, isn't it?" she said, and when he answered in his quiet manner, "Yes, it's a grand country," she felt that he saw it as she did, in all its splendor and tranquillity.

After a time he began to talk about the *Macon*, whose construction he had studied, and went on from that to the rearmament program, and to the possible future usefulness of lighter-than-air craft. He talked easily, as if to someone whom he had known a long time, and yet with an engaging shyness. He was entirely unassuming. She let him choose his topics, only putting in a word now and then to keep the conversation going, but she could not escape observing that everything he said might have been said by John, that he had lived, it seemed, the life she would have imagined for her son. But he presented it to her more fully than she could have imagined it, just as she could not have imagined this particular combination of her own features and those of her husband, this face of a new individual. Her affection went out toward him powerfully, with a great sense of gratitude, as if her own son had indeed been returned to her briefly, through some miracle. And as she listened to his voice, and watched the sun withdrawing, gleam after gleam, from the fields, then from the eastern mountains, the recollection of having felt like this another time, and more than once, before, returned to her and would not be dispelled.

The recollections were distinct enough, now. This was not the first time that she had met an individual, a boy, sometimes of one age, sometimes of another, who resembled John, and the boy, as now, always the exact age that John would have been, had he lived. Tom had called it her bad habit of seeing ghosts in broad daylight. He had not been unsympathetic; and she had tried each time to consider the strange experience with common sense and even with some humor. It had happened three times before, and the last time had been so long ago, five—or was it six?—years ago, that she had thought it would never happen again, certainly not in all its strangeness.

Although there had been something disturbing, even frightening, in connection with each of these encounters, there had never been anything which could not be explained naturally. If Sara McDermott saw ghosts, she saw them rationally. And on this early winter afternoon she was aware of nothing about her encounter with the soldier which, extraordinary as the resemblance seemed, could not be reasonably accounted for, or which she need find disturbing. There was nothing which need link this meeting with the others, she argued, and felt justified in her attempt to put the more disturbing aspects of the earlier experiences from her mind.

The fact, however, remained that, shadowed slightly by those other encounters and reinforced by her ever-living love for her lost son, this meeting with a young stranger had assumed a special meaning for her, and that the afternoon had already become one which she would remember all her life, with special tenderness, with special gratitude.

Sara McDermott would not for the world have intruded this deep emotion of hers upon her guest—for he was her guest, although not in her house. The casualness of the relationship was a part of its charm. It gave her the replica of her son as he would have been if she had been happily in touch with him through all these years, the image of an intimacy which was not weighted by the repeated sense of loss which she had known. And as they rode on in the isolation of the moving car she blessed the chance encounter and turned her attention wholly toward appreciating what chance had given her. It did not occur to her to try to extend the meeting beyond the allotted twenty minutes or so which the journey to San Jose would give her. She did not even want to ask him his name. But she received most happily the disconnected, cheerful stream of anecdotes about his boyhood, his plans, his observations of things and people and animals with which he unostentatiously returned her hospitality.

Dusk had descended upon them as they reached the outskirts of Santa Clara, and as they passed the big dark shapes of cannery buildings and entered the shadows of eucalyptus windbreaks, she switched on the headlights. The increased traffic in Santa Clara made talking a little difficult. They lapsed into an easy silence, and the darkness, obliterating the landscape, closed them in a more complete privacy—or so it seemed to Sara McDermott. It was still early, not yet six o'clock, but once the sun was gone the darkness increased rapidly. There was no lingering twilight. The outskirts of Santa Clara blended unnoticeably with those of San Jose, and they were well into the latter town before Sara remarked:

"You'll be arriving at Carmel very late, even with the best of luck."

"Oh, I shan't mind that," said the boy. "But you mustn't take me any farther. This has been swell. You'd better drop me off now."

She began to look for a place in which to park, but the avenue was crowded—streetcars, busses, Saturday-night shoppers. She turned, after a block or so, to a side street, and there managed to find a place next to the curb. She stopped the car and turned to the soldier. He had opened the door and reached one foot out to the pavement. Then he turned and, putting both hands over hers, leaned toward her.

"Good-bye, darling," he said, and kissed her on the mouth.

For Sara McDermott it seemed at that moment as if the wall between the hereafter and the now, the impenetrable, inexorable wall between the living and the dead, had melted like mist in the sun. For that moment her John, her own son, held his living hands upon hers. The hands were warm, and so was the gentle kiss. Then he was gone, and she sat there, surrounded by the darkness full of noises of traffic and of people hurrying past, convinced as she had never been convinced before of the complete possibility of the return of the dead. She knew then, for that moment, that he had visited her before. Those other times—they had not been illusions. It had always been John himself, no counterfeit, no surprising resemblance, but her boy, himself.

Her first thought, when she could think at all beyond the awareness of the great revelation, was that she must not let him go. He came so seldom—four times only in all his life; and he was so beloved. Mechanically she withdrew the key from the lock and slipped it into her pocket, and left the car. Upon the pavement the lights and shadows from the stores were cut and interrupted by shapes of passers-by, all indistinguishable in the night. She turned first in one direction, then in the other, wondering which way he had taken. She must find him; she could drive him all the way to Carmel. She must not lose him now. She turned finally toward the main street, hurrying, because she had no idea of how long she had been sitting there in the car after he left her. It had seemed only a moment, but it must have been much longer because she could see no glimpse of him. When she reached the avenue, with its greater illumination, she looked up and down the pavements again, and then, seeing a policeman standing at the corner with a whistle in his hand, walked up to him.

She stood looking up at him, for she was not a tall woman, while he directed the crowd at the crossing; and when he looked down at her at last, she said, "Did you see a soldier just now?"

"A soldier?" returned the cop genially. "Lady, I seen six or a dozen soldiers in the last minute and a half. This town is lousy with soldiers."

"Oh," she said, feeling like several kinds of a fool. Her disappointment, verging on despair, must have been all too evident.

The policeman said kindly, as if to a child, "What kind of a soldier?"

"Oh," she answered lamely, "a young soldier. A flier. I'm sorry. I thought he might be waiting at this corner."

She made her way back to the car, walking through darkness grown physical, as if it impeded her progress, and seated again behind the wheel, safe in privacy, she bowed her head on her hands. It was happening just as it had happened all the other times—first the tremendous joy of recognition, then the terrible premonition of disaster. He had come to her, as he had come those other times, at that moment when, had he lived, he should again be leaving her; at that moment when, had he lived, he would again have to die, that moment when the wall between the hereafter and the now grew thin, and melted. Then, because she loved him and remembered him at all times, whether consciously or not, he returned to her. If he had lived all those rich twenty-one years, lived to have all those good memories and plans of which he had just now been speaking to her, the time had come when he would have to leave her, and leave this rich and fortunate life. But, she thought, the premonition crowding upon her, who else will have to die now with him? Because that is the way it has always happened. Because only the first time would I have been alone in my loss.

Someone tapped on the window of the car on the side toward the curbing and then opened the door. The policeman, bending in order to see into the car, asked her, "Are you sick, lady?"

"Sick?" she echoed, startled, returning his worried stare. "Oh no. Perfectly all right. Really."

"Well," he said apologetically, "you looked so queer a minute ago, I thought maybe I could help you."

"I'm perfectly all right," she assured him firmly. She dug into her pocket for the keys. "I was just wondering what to do next." She must have been convincing, for he straightened and said with a slight laugh:

"Okay, lady. But you gimme a turn."

"Thanks," she said. "Thanks for bothering, but please shut the door. I must be getting along."

She began to retrace her journey, but alone. The conversation with the policeman had jolted her. She said to herself, "See here, Sara McDermott, you are making a ghost of a perfectly healthy young man, and be thankful he didn't know what foolishness has been going on in your head. It was decent of the cop not to think I was drunk." But when she had driven through the darkness for perhaps another five minutes the sense of impending disaster had returned so strongly that she all but cried out, "What can I do to avert it?"

Nothing, her memory answered. The other times you were always too late, and this time you do not even know in which direction to turn to look for what is coming. A flier. A bomber pilot. A crash in a training plane. A crash of the next car in which he may be given a lift. A death by drowning in the sea, at Carmel. A fall over the cliffs. But he would not be alone. He was never alone, after the first time.

The turmoil in her mind did not extend itself to her hands. She drove steadily, expertly; she was not trembling. She felt perfectly well, and physically very, very capable. But she was baffled. With all her energy, there was nothing she could do. Not this time.

The last time? The last time she had tried, at least. It was something to have tried. The time before—she had tried then too, but the first time she had not understood what it was that she was facing. It had begun so long ago. Driving now through the cool and spacious darkness toward her home, the refuge of her spirit as well as of her body, she reflected that all her life had been bound into this one adventure. All her life, ever since the birth of John, the last twenty-one years, although she had gone about the practical business of living with courage and good sense, although she had been greatly interested in Tom's career and proud of his professional triumphs, although she had taken great interest in dozens of younger people, although she seemed to forget, and had upon occasion even tried to forget them, these meetings with her boy, this sense of the continuity of John's life, running along somehow parallel in time with her own, had been her real life and her own adventure.

She had not been dismally unhappy all these years. She had not brooded over her loss, or consciously tried to recall each day just how old John would then have been; but she had measured his life by the lives of other living children, and she had rejoiced in the other children too. And there had never been anything to bear witness to an outsider of the true inwardness of the affair. It had always been, just as now, perfectly reasonable. The soldier had vanished. But of course the town had been, as the policeman had remarked, lousy with soldiers. He might have stepped into any one of half a dozen stores. He might have picked up another lift. And yet, Sara McDermott would have testified before the court of heaven that evening, that if every soldier in the

state of California had been mustered at that hour, the
soldier whom she had seen would not have been of their
number.

At home, at the end of her twenty-minute drive, she
switched on the light in the familiar living room and
laid her handbag on the round table under the walnut-
framed mirror where Tom had left the papers for her to
correct and type. She looked at herself in the mirror, as
if she half expected to see herself changed. But the dark
eyes regarded her with faint amusement, practical and
steady in their gaze. Her face was neither more nor less
lined than it had appeared that afternoon. Her hair was
disarranged by the wind, and that was all. She said to her
reflection, "You don't look like a woman who would be
seeing ghosts by daylight, or any other way," and turned
aside to proceed with the evening routine.

She set about keeping her promise to Tom. The papers
demanded concentration, and the habit of keeping prom-
ises held her mind to them until the last page was folded
and tucked into the long envelope.

Before she locked the front door she stood on the doorstep, looking into the darkness. Stars were out. She
noticed Orion low in the southern sky. The air was clear,
but so mild that it seemed as if a south wind might spring
up at any moment, bringing rain. So she closed all the
south windows, conscientiously, thinking that Tom was
usually the careful householder who made the last round
of the premises at night, and in thinking so, wished
tremendously that he were there and that she might re-
late to his sensible ear the details of her last meeting
with her ghost. The sense of imminent disaster was so
strong that she felt she would almost have been willing

to sacrifice her glimpse of her boy in order not to feel
that so much sorrow was in store for another woman. For
that was what it had come to. The visitation had always
meant the death of someone other than John. Her husband would listen with his quiet understanding gaze,
and, without making fun of her, draw her back to the
sanity of every day.

"For I must be a little insane," she thought.

Lying in bed, with a glimpse of the night sky beyond
the thin branches of the prune tree by the window, she
tried to escape from that sense of impending grief and,
thinking of the candid and friendly face of the soldier,
tried to remember only the sweetness of the encounter.
She slept, and dreamed, and woke to remember earlier,
happier days, and slept uneasily again.

It had all begun so long ago. Perhaps, had she counted
less upon the birth of that child to recompense her for
other losses, she might have felt the loss of the infant less
deeply. Perhaps it was the strength of that initial sorrow
that had kept her linked mysteriously with the spirit of
that lost child. Two months before the birth of John both
her parents had been killed in an auto accident. It had
been a great shock; the sense of needless loss had made
her rebellious. But remembering the child whom she
carried beneath her heart, she had refused to give way to
her emotion. She had told herself that life was continu-
ous, and that the child would be no less the inheritor of
the qualities which she had loved in his grandparents
for being born at a time when they could no longer be
there to welcome him. She told herself that he would
restore to her something of her father and mother, as well
as be bringing her a new version of Tom, and he was,

unborn, a comrade to her, and a great consolation through those two difficult months.

The night that he was born was not much milder than this night, but it was spring in Illinois, and, going out to the car by starlight, she had passed under the pink and white blossoms of the crabapple tree and had breathed their fragrance. And all the way in to the hospital she had felt joyous, as she had not felt in all those two months, a joy unforced and not to be diminished by any memory of death or any prospect of suffering. It had never occurred to her that the child would not live.

The loss was absolute, for her physician explained to her that it would not be possible for her to bear another child. She had not made a fuss about the situation. That would have been too hard on Tom, who was as disappointed as herself. She promptly gave away all the things which she had prepared for the child and turned to being Tom's devoted secretary as well as housekeeper. And the years had not been unhappy, not in the long run. Tom had been too grand a person for that; and life had been full; life had been interesting; there had been other children, Judy's children, and other children still. And there had been the "ghost."

Judy, her cousin, had a little boy a half year older than John would have been. When she returned to Kensington, to live within a few blocks of Tom and Sara, she had brought the baby for Sara to look after, during those first distracted days of moving in. A jolly, capable child he had been, who sat up with a fine straight back upon the blanket which Judy spread on the floor for him, and looked about him with unastonished but interested blue eyes. Sara, dropping on her knees to bring her countenance on a level with his, looked at him with delight.

"Isn't it surprising," she said to Judy, "how they take everything so calmly? Strange houses, strange cousins, and all that. Or is it just the way you brought him up? He's wonderful, Judy."

"Oh, Sally," said her cousin, "you're swell. I ought to apologize, but I've been scared of having you see him. For fear you'd resent him. Me having him, and you not having—the other one."

"What do you take me for, Judy?" said Sara.

"I'm sorry, Sally. I really did know better. But if it had been me instead of you, I might have gone sour on everything."

Why she had not gone sour Sara did not know. Perhaps it was Tom's steadying comradeship. Perhaps it had been because of her good health, which had permitted her to work hard at other interests. She did not feel inclined to take much credit to herself for it. But at any rate, from that day on, the small cousin had been partly hers. She had adored him, and the fact that the pleasure of caring for him was in a way vicarious did not blight it. She was thankful for him. Judy's second child, a daughter, born when the boy was only two, gave Sara more of his company. And it was good to know that she was a help to Judy, because Judy and she had been great friends ever since they had been in grammar school together.

There was always a small chair in the McDermott living room for the little boy, and in the garden there was a pool with turtles. Tom made the pool, and Tom put up the swing under the oak tree, but Sara shopped for the turtles. The small cousin grew apace. He was like

Judy, tall and lean, with sudden blue eyes, and much given to climbing. He liked to be read to, also, and Sara had made room on a low shelf for books that were his. And then, when he was four, and a little over, he was sent to kindergarten every morning on a bus with a crowd of his contemporaries, because Judy was a firm believer in awakening the social consciousness early. He took to it happily, but Sara found that she missed his morning visits.

One morning in the autumn of that year Sara was in her yard planting tulip bulbs. New people were moving in next door, and beyond the hedge she could catch glimpses now and then of chairs and tables standing on the lawn with other household gear, while there was much coming and going between the front door and the moving van at the curb. She worked away with her trowel at the brown earth, thinking that before long the earth would be hard with frost, and dug her holes deep, evenly spaced in concentric ovals. The tulip bulbs lay beside her in an old wicker flower basket. She was presently aware of being watched, and lifted her head to see a small, fair-haired boy standing beside her. He was sturdily built, and his pink cheeks were so round that when he smiled the corners of his eyes seemed almost to slant upward, dark eyes, very dark and bright in his fair little face, and rather elfish because of the upward tilt at the corners. He was not any child whom she had ever seen before. He must belong to the strangers who were moving in next door, she thought. He had probably come through the gap in the hedge. And since the grass had been raked that morning there had been no rustle of oak leaves to announce his approach.

He stood looking down at her and smiling, and as she resumed her work he watched, following the motions of her hands with his eyes but not saying anything. When all the holes were ready, she turned to the basket of bulbs and, selecting a few, turned them about in her hands, brushed off loose flakes of skin.

"They look like onions, don't they?" she said to her visitor. "But they're not. They're flowers. They will be lovely red flowers, like cups, when spring comes, on long tall stems. You'll see."

She set them one by one in the holes and packed the earth firmly and gently above them. The little boy, after the bed was half planted, crouched down and put his hand in the basket of bulbs, following her example. Charmed, Sara indicated with her trowel which holes should be planted next, and the small hand deposited the bulbs carefully, one in each hole.

"No, wait," said Sara, laughing. "Not upside down. See, they have tops and bottoms to them. If you plant one like that, upside down, the poor little stem will have to grow out at the bottom and curl all the way around before it can start to grow up and into the sunshine. This way." She set the bulb as it should be and, smiling at the child, continued, "They're going to grow, you know, not go to sleep. They'll be here asleep all winter while the snow comes down, but in the spring they'll wake up and begin to grow."

The child listened, smiling, but did not say anything. He helped her fill in the holes, and, when the entire bed had been planted, he watched her rake the brown oak leaves thick over it.

"I expect, when he begins to talk, he'll babble like a

mountain brook," she thought. His silence was so full of co-operation that she was in no hurry to have him break it. She was sure now that he must belong next door, because there was nothing of the lost child about him. He was perfectly happy. He gazed about her yard with interest, his little upward-slanting dark eyes so bright that they verged upon the mischievous. He saw the swing, and by tacit consent they walked over to it together, and presently she was swinging him, pushing his solid little back with the palms of her hands so that he flew away from her in a long arc, then back, to meet her hands, then out again.

He was a trifle younger than Judy's boy, she guessed—not so tall, but solider. He probably weighed a good bit more. What a nice pair they'd make, and how jolly it was going to be to have him for a neighbor! She wished she could have him entirely, keep him, just as he was. Why, already she felt as if she had known him all his life. When he tired of the swing, looking over his shoulder to tell her, with his eyes, that he was ready for something else, she said, "Turtles," and, that being quite adequate, he put his hand in hers and they went to visit the pond.

The water was cold this morning, still in shadow, and the turtles were in hiding. She stooped down beside him, searching for them, until they both saw the small, pointed dark head resting its chin upon two little black paws at the edge of a water hyacinth, while the turtle floated half submerged. Sara scooped the animal from the water expertly, the head and tail and legs all disappearing rapidly within the shell as she held it dripping. The little boy reached out his hands for it, and she laid the wet black box of shell with its cold mysterious inhabitant upon the small unflinching palms.

"He's not the kind that bites, of course," she said, although the child did not need her reassurance. His head inclined intently above the treasure, he stood perfectly still, as if forgetful of her presence, and she observed how the thick soft silvery hair pushed to one side at a natural crown, not parted, let show through it faintly the pink of his scalp—a suggestion of pale rose, almost an iridescence. Judy's child last summer had tanned clear to the roots of his hair, running about hatless, but this child was one of those absolute blonds who never tan, who burn, perhaps, or freckle, but who never really tan. Tom was another such. She thought how Tom would take to a young fellow who held a turtle with such fine unsqueamish curiosity. The child looked up suddenly, throwing back his head to meet her downward gaze, and announced, quite irrelevantly:

"I go to school now."

It was rather a low voice for so young a child, low in register, but clear and firm, and he pronounced his words as if each one were of definite importance to him, slighting none of the letters.

"Do you?" said Sara quickly. "I guess you like it too, don't you?" But the child had resumed his contemplation of the turtle, which was tentatively extending its head, turned to one side, so that one eye was exposed before the whole head was out. The child had said his say and was again wholly concerned with the creature on his palm. Sara looked down at him, smiling unconsciously, stirred to the depths of her heart by his oblivious charm, by his entire suitability for herself and for Tom.

He was, of all the small children she had ever met, the one she would most have liked to have for her own.

As they stood thus, the child absorbed in the turtle and Sara in the child, a delivery wagon rattled into the McDermott driveway with a screech of its brakes and precipitated, as it were, upon the side doorstep a lively driver, who pounded upon the door, and then, seeing Sara McDermott in the distance, hallooed to her to come and receive her bundle of laundry. She left the child with a promise to be back in a moment, and relieved the laundryman of his package. When she approached the door she heard the phone ringing, and as she stepped inside to lay the bundle on a chair it continued to ring with what struck her as annoying and unusual persistence. The voice that met her ear was Tom's, and he began without preliminary.

"You must go over to Judy at once," he said.

"What is the matter?" she asked.

"The child," he said. "The kindergarten bus. An accident."

"A bad one?"

"About as bad as could be," the voice answered inexorably, and continued, in Tom's steadiest tones, "The bus was crossing the Slow-water at the Elm Street bridge. Nobody knows yet how it happened. The driver went straight through the rail. And into the river. They are getting some of them out. Some of them are drowned. It's too early to know how many."

"Judy's?"

"Yes," said the voice. "He was way up at the front. It went in head first. You must get over to Judy's right away." He hung up abruptly, and she knew all at once that he must be one of those who were helping. He had telephoned from near the bridge. He hadn't time to wait to see how she took the news herself.

She went in a dreadful mechanical daze to her room, found her purse and the keys to the car, hooked the front screen door, and left the house by the side door, as she had entered it, a few minutes earlier. Her first thought even then was to say good-bye to her small visitor, but she did not see him standing by the pool as she came out. She made a few steps from the driveway, looking for him, and then concluded that he must have slipped back to his own yard through the gap in the hedge. As she started the car and backed down the driveway, which the laundryman had vacated immediately upon the completion of his errand, she thought with an odd sense of comfort that when this dreadful morning was over she might return and find him again. She would call upon his mother the very first free moment she could find. He would not help Judy much, she supposed, this small new neighbor of hers, but he would be an infinite consolation to herself.

Years afterward she remembered the distress of that day. No grief that she had ever borne herself, it seemed to her, had ever caused her as great pain as having to explain to Judy what had happened and having to live with Judy each hour which increased the realization of the disaster and its unalterableness. Tom had been right to send her. Because she had been through disaster herself, as well as because she had loved the drowned boy almost as much as his mother did, Judy could accept her, and accept from her such practical advice as Sara could offer. She could not have accepted it from another.

The long day was ended finally, with the baby girl fed and bathed and put to sleep, Judy in bed, asleep under the influence of a sedative, and Judy's husband home to take over the responsibility of the house for the night. Sara would be back early in the morning.

She found Tom at home when she returned. She could see the silhouette of his square figure in the lighted window, waiting for her, but as she was about to enter the house she caught sight of the shadowy figure of a woman on the lawn beyond the hedge. So she continued down the driveway, and down the sidewalk to her neighbor's gate. The woman on the lawn came forward to meet her, holding the evening paper in her hand, still furled. She had evidently just come outdoors in order to find it.

"Good evening," said Sara McDermott.

"Good evening," said the woman, polite interrogation in the words.

"I am your neighbor," said Sara. "I thought I'd just like to say a word of welcome, and to congratulate you on having such a charming young son."

"A son?" said the woman, surprised. "But we don't have any children." She had come close enough now so that through the dusk Sara could see her face, a face rather lined, rather thin, but pleasant, under a cloud of gray hair.

"Oh, but he came to call on me this morning when you were moving in," said Sara. "A little boy, about four, with a lot of fair hair. Doesn't he live with you?"

"No," said the woman, polite but pleasant, a little puzzled by Sara's definite conviction. "No little boy of any sort lives with us. I'm sure I haven't seen any little boy around here today."

She waited for Sara to say good night and move on, but since Sara did not move and only stared at her, looking baffled and hurt, she suggested, "Perhaps he lives across the street. I don't know any of the children in the neighborhood as yet."

"No," said Sara. "He doesn't belong to the neighborhood. I know every child for blocks around."

"Well," said the woman, "perhaps he was lost."

"He didn't look lost," said Sara McDermott, as if she were releasing a long sigh with the words, and, without further comment or amenity, dropped her hand from her neighbor's gate and went home.

Her conversation with Tom that evening was almost entirely about Judy. They were both thankful for the existence of the little girl.

"It'll pull her through," said Tom.

The cause of the accident had not yet been determined, but it was supposed that it might have been defective steering gear. The driver of the bus had been a dependable man. There was no reason why, upon turning from the boulevard to the bridge, he should have continued to turn until he swung completely over the edge of the bridge, crashing through the wooden railing. What had saved most of the children was the fact that the bus had a door at the back, and the door had not been submerged.

Sara McDermott spent the whole of the next day with Judy, tending the baby, washing, cooking, answering phone calls, sorting laundry, picking up all the various threads of Judy's housekeeping. Judy was still in bed.

And as Sara worked there persisted the hope behind everything she did that when she returned home that evening she might find the fair-haired little boy in her yard. She stopped beside the pool late that afternoon, just where the child had stood, bending his head above the turtle in his hand, and wished with an immense and almost unaccountable tenderness that she could see him again if only for a few minutes.

She mentioned him to Tom after supper that night, as they sat finishing their coffee at the table in the kitchen. She said, after she had recounted the whole interview and had added the statement of the woman next door that she had no children:

"He looked so much like you, Tom, so much as you must have looked when you were little." She lifted her eyes shyly from the consideration of her cup, which she had been setting precisely in the center of its saucer. "It seems to me now that he must have been Johnny himself, come alive in some miraculous way. Can you touch a ghost, Tom?"

"I've always heard that was one of the things you couldn't do," he answered.

"Then he wasn't a ghost," said Sara. "I never touched a solider little back."

"Didn't he tell you his name, or anything?" asked Tom.

"He never said a word the whole time," Sara answered, "until just before the laundryman came. Then he said, 'I go to school now.'"

She stopped, because she could not bear to present to Tom the thought which then entered her mind: *"If Johnny had lived to be four years old, he would have been with Judy's child, on that bus, and we should have*

lost him all over again." The image of the child in the
garden became completely and unchangeably then the
image of Johnny as he would have been had he lived.
She had never been able to imagine how he would have
looked. Knowing, from Judy's children, how unpredict-
able, how entirely unimaginable the face of a child can
be, even when all the elements of inheritance are plainly
readable in the new face, she had never tried to visualize
the face of her son. Now she knew that he would always
wear, for her, the face of the child by the pool. She said,
because Tom was waiting for her to go on speaking,
"Well, I should have liked him for a ghost. So I can't
have him for one?"

"He'll probably turn up again," said Tom, "solider
than ever."

But he did not turn up again. Sara's inquiries about the
neighborhood never yielded any clue to his identity, and
when she mentioned him again to Tom, some weeks
later, he suggested that the child had probably been with
people who were motoring through Kensington, on their
way to Chicago.

"We get more transients in this village than you
realize," he said.

Sara did not speak of him again to Tom, and she had
never mentioned him to Judy. She put the memory of
him away in the part of her mind where she kept certain
memories of Tom when she had first begun to fall in
love, of the spring night on which John had been born,
a few memories of her childhood, of standing at the edge
of the flooded woods on a spring evening, memories kept
without the benefit of words.

Judy's sorrow was slowly absorbed by the routine of

living. After a few years she bore another son, and two years after, another, so that her family consisted of a seven-year-old daughter with two little brothers. Tom and Sara left Kensington for Detroit, where Tom's business took him, and Sara and Judy exchanged such letters as cousins manage to find time for, penciled notes, scribbled at the day's end, or while the roast was cooking. Tom's success as a designer of cabin cruisers astonished himself. Those were the years in which there were customers for luxury yachts. His stanch craft were small and manageable, and ready for anything from Lake Superior to the Gulf Stream. Of course designing yachts was hardly the same as owning them, but there was enough new prosperity so that Sara felt justified in inviting Judy and all three children to spend the summer with her at the island in northern Michigan. Tom was planning to commute between Detroit and the island, as business permitted, and perhaps Judy's husband could also come north for a few weeks in September.

The place had belonged to Sara's father and mother and was rich in memories, and, although she loved it, she did not like the prospect of being alone there for long stretches at a time. Short stretches were all right, she thought, as she breakfasted alone on the long veranda the morning after her arrival. For a few days it would be pleasant to come upon happy and touching recollections as she swept out the winter's dust—what little dust there was in that region of leaf and water—and shook out blankets, and emptied bureau drawers.

She had come early in order to arrange things at her leisure, to get in groceries, and set up extra cots for the children, and have white bunchberry blossoms and a few early clusters of red bunchberries, too, in the green pottery bowl on the brick mantel. And also, she reflected honestly, in order to have to herself these recollections that started up from corners, that lurked in the kitchen cupboards and at the door to the boathouse.

It was late June. She brushed away a few mosquitoes as she ate her toast and marmalade. Later the mosquitoes would all be gone—that was one of the blessings of being so far north. Across the river the Canadian fields sunned themselves, green and tranquil, and she could hear the bells of cows she could not see, and hear the splashing of hoofs as they entered the river on the Canadian shore to drink. The water must be awfully cold yet, fresh from Superior. She would not care to try a morning swim for another week or two, at least. It was going to be nice for Judy's children. Judy had been here once, before she was married. Sara searched her memory for the year. How long ago! It was the summer before their senior year in high school.

Sara took great pleasure in shifting the furniture about, in sorting linens and portioning out the warm bedding. "If Tom leaves me an impoverished widow someday I believe I'll open a hotel," she said to herself, without any expectation whatever of such a contingency's ever arising, but merely because she did like the practical side of keeping house. She planned to let the little girl sleep on the porch.

"She will love that," thought Sara, "just as I did, waking to see the first sun coming through the leaves and the river rippling and bright—and then being able to tell the boys that she was first person up."

At noon she had a glass of milk and a sandwich, and

a short visit with the man who brought the milk and ice
by rowboat from his farm up the river, and ordered extra
milk against the day of the children's arrival. About two
o'clock she decided to let the grand dishwashing go until
tomorrow—the field mice had been traipsing among the
cups and saucers—and tomorrow she would also take the
kerosene stove apart and clean it. The wood stove was in
good order, and the warmth would be welcome in the
evening. And meanwhile the sun had grown warm, and
it seemed too bad not to be outdoors. She set out in the
direction of the post office, although she knew the mail
would not be along for several hours.

The pathway, used only by the few people who stayed
the winter through at the island, had an untrodden look.
Later, in August, when all the cottagers had arrived, it
would be widened, and beaten harder, and the flowers
beside it would not look so fresh. How well she remembered this early-season look of it, and all its windings!
She walked without haste, enjoying this communion
with earlier summers, glad that the cottages she passed
were still boarded up, and glad to think that later they
would be opened, and former neighbors would be returned, people whom Judy would enjoy meeting. The
first cottage about which she saw any signs of habitation
was the old house below the Point, and she saw it from
the crest of the hill behind it.

There was a thin thread of smoke coming from the
living-room chimney, the one to the west. She stood
looking down for a time upon the gray roofs, for the
house was built in an ell, the western part being much
older than the rest, and upon the river beyond it, and the
Canadian shore, closer here to the American than it was

farther upstream. The Coast Guard station at the Point
had a fresh coat of paint, white on the walls, bright red
on the roof, and she could see, even from the hill, how
the turn of the river had dug into the nearer bank.
Formerly there had been a footpath between the fence
and the river. Now the fence overhung the bank pre-
cariously.

She turned back into the woods and found the bracken
knee-deep among the poplars—popples, they called them
locally—so that the path was almost lost. The popples,
too, had grown since she was last there. They almost
screened the old barn which had belonged to the house
below, when it was a homestead and not a summer cottage.

The barn was of logs, hewn square and silvered by the
snow. In the doorway, from which the door had long
since been removed, there was a huge silver wasp nest.
It might have been untenanted, but she did not inquire.
Instead she sat down in the dry sunny grass, the broad
ferns interspersed with long-stemmed buttercups, and
then lay down, because the ground was warm and
springy. It was quiet. There wasn't a sound except the
twirling of the poplar leaves in an imperceptible wind.
It had always been like this, years ago.

She heard the boy coming along the path and sat up.
He was whistling, without much tune. He might have
been nine years old, and he came directly to her, dropping down beside her in the grass with an amusing grin
that made the corners of his eyes seem to slant slightly
upward. His eyes were very dark, his hair cut short and
very fair. His nose was peeling from sunburn. He must
have been on the river the day before. Only on the water,

fishing for hours, could he have got such a sunburn so early in the season. So she said, "How's the fishing?"

"Swell," he answered promptly. "I got a musky at the Dumps. Absolutely—it wasn't a pike. We counted the scales. It was all of eleven pounds. My first musky."

"Did it fight?" she asked.

"Not a bit. Came in like a log. And we conked it with the crank right away. It was all over before I could get excited. But it *was* a musky. I always knew I could catch one if I could get out before July."

She remembered her own first, and only, muskellunge, and understood why he had stopped to talk. Naturally he had to talk about it, and there were so few people here yet that he must have had only his family for an audience so far. But who was he? She knew all of the families with farms near the island—the natives, as the summer people called them, who in turn called the summer people tourists, to the chagrin of some of them who had been "tourists" for thirty years in a row. No, he was one of the cottagers, but it must be a family new since her last visit. He was probably from the house at the foot of the hill. She did not inquire because he had, in fellowship, asked her if she had ever caught a musky.

"Yes," she said, honored by the question, "but it wasn't as big as yours and it was in September, all the wrong time, of course. I was sure it was a pike, but Charlie Stuart said it was a musky. He was just coming along with the ice when we got home with it and—I can see him yet—I had to have him look over my catch. You know Charlie?"

"Of course," he said. "Indian Charlie. Was he around then?"

"He's always been around, but he isn't Indian."

"I know," said the boy, "but he talks Indian, and we call him Indian Charlie. Did he ever tell you about the time he froze his feet? That's why he walks so stumpy."

"The time he ran aground above Two Tree Island in a sailboat, and it snowed that night?"

"That's it," he said. "It's a swell story, the way he tells it, isn't it? He knows lots of swell stories. He doesn't like pike. You can give pike to the O'Tooles because there're so many of them, but Charlie sticks for perch and bass *and* musky."

"But I remember," said Sara slowly, reaching toward two memories at once, "I remember it was Indian Charlie who showed us how to smoke a pike."

The boy was interested, and she had to explain the method to him at once. He was all for consulting Charlie himself the next time he should meet him. But as she talked Sara was remembering also the small boy at the pool in Kensington—that was it—the four-year-old with the turtle in the palm of his hand. He had eyes like this boy, and, given five years, he might have grown as much. She felt for this boy the same quick, delighted comradeship that she had felt for that smaller one, planting the tulip bulb upside down. What a difference five years could make!

But the boy was standing up, unlimbering his legs.

"I get pins and needles in my foot awful easy," he said, looking down at her, and then, "I've got to go now. I'm going swimming at the Point with a fellow and he'll be waiting for me."

"At the Point?" said Sara. "But that's the coldest place on the shore."

"Sure," said the boy with his companionable grin, "but the water's deep, too. You can dive off the bank."

He was gone without further ado, no prolonged farewell such as an adult might have felt necessary in order to avoid rudeness. He simply walked off through the poplars, toward the crest of the hill, the bracken switching about his legs as he went, his back broad and sturdy at the shoulders, narrow at the hips, the sunlight shining unsteadily on his cropped fair head.

He had disappeared completely before Sara got to her feet. It was the same boy, or if it wasn't, what did it matter? He was so jolly that she wasn't going to lose him as quickly as all this. She started through the poplars after him. He must have broken into a run, for she did not catch up with him or even with a glimpse of him. She came out of the trees on the edge of the hill and did not see him anywhere. Then she remembered how the path to the Point curved back through the cedar woods to avoid the steep descent of the hill, and she turned back toward the path, losing sight of the shore and of the river.

The cedars were shadowy, very different from the popple grove. The path broadened. It had been a logging road once.

"I wish he were not going to swim at the Point," she said aloud. "It's dangerous." Then the premonition of disaster came upon her, far deeper than the shadows among the cedars, and she began to run. She remembered that the little boy by the pool had been a visitant just before the wreck of the kindergarten bus. She had no time to argue with herself about the existence of ghosts. She was very frightened, and she ran. Fortunately the way was downhill. She came from the cedars a hundred yards or so above the Point, where the woods broke down into sumach bushes and wild roses, and she could see the Coast Guard station, and farther to the right, really quite far to the right, the fence and the yard of the old house. The cove, where the boys would be swimming, was hidden from her by the station. She stopped running, and walked, but only because she was out of breath.

When she came to the shore she found the Coast Guard man standing at the edge of the landing float. She knew him, of course. He was Peter Rousseau. She said as she came out on the float beside him, "The kids oughtn't to swim here. It's no bathing beach."

His face, as he turned to her, told her that she had come too late.

"I've been telling him that for the last week," said Rousseau. "The damn little fool would dive off the bank. This time he must have got a cramp. Or struck his head. He hasn't come up, and it's too long."

"What are you doing about it?" she asked.

"What can I do?" he returned in anger that was not directed against her, she knew. "I hailed Charlie. I can't dive for him. Would if I could."

She saw then that Indian Charlie was there with his rowboat, holding to the lower rung of the big light at the turn of the channel, and she saw also the massive swift approach of an ore barge. From a distance the freighters seemed to creep, but here at the Point, where the shore was close to the channel, the speed with which they moved was evident, and terrifying. All the water in the cove rushed out to meet the bulk of the freighter, a strange phenomenon, as if the river rose to float the big ship. It had always been like that. "How much does she draw?" you inquired about a boat, and here at the Point the freighters seemed to draw the entire river toward them. The freighter signaled, one long blast, required by the law at the Point to warn the shipping farther up the channel. The noise filled the air, deafening, absorbing; it was impossible to think or feel until the noise died away. Then the boat began to swing in its almost right-angled turn, the stern swinging, the prow seeming stationary, the stern and meantime the great length sliding past with a subdued rush of engines and disturbed water. Charlie Stuart hung fast to the base of the light, his small boat swinging toward the freighter, like a needle to a magnet. When the freighter had passed, and the boiling water of her wake had subsided into smooth green swells, he released his grip on the ladder and took to his oars again, cruising downstream, nearer the shore. Rousseau and Sara McDermott watched him with the fascination of despair. Rousseau turned away first, remembering his job, and went into the station to record the passing of the *Joseph T. Flannery* of Duluth at three-five. When he came out again he said to Sara:

"Someone will have to go tell his mother. She's in the old house there—new this season. I doubt you've met her yet, have you?"

"I only got here last night, Pete," she said. "This is the first I've been away from the cabin. Do you say she's new here?"

"Oh yes," he replied. "They're friends of the Hudsons, just up from Flint for the first time."

"But the boy seemed to know his way around these

parts," said Sara. "He talked like an old-timer. I met him up by the old barn."

"When was that?" said Pete.

"Just now, about ten minutes ago."

"Couldn't have been the same boy," said Pete. "He was here almost all afternoon with me, fooling around and asking questions about the boats. He went home to get in his swimming suit and came right back. I told him not to swim here."

"But there were two boys. The one I saw was a towhead about nine years old."

Pete Rousseau shook his head. "This one's as dark as I am."

"Then what became of the other one?" said Sara.

"There wasn't any other," said Pete with slight impatience. "Just this kid from Flint, name of Bettenger. Someone's got to speak to his mother. I'm not supposed to leave the station. Won't you go, please, Mrs. McDermott? Maybe Charlie'll go with you."

Sara knew that he was relieved to remember that he ought not to leave the station; and of course he was right. He was on duty. He signaled to Charlie Stuart, who pulled slowly toward them, keeping as close to the shore as he could to avoid the push of the current. It was swift water, swift and heavy. The stake which marked the Canadian edge of the channel was bowed halfway to the surface of the river by the weight of it, and it pushed up against the base of the light before dividing and swirling past, downstream. It was a perfectly crazy place for a child to swim, a child who did not know the river. Of course she had swum there herself when she was a kid, but wasn't that before they deepened the channel? She understood now why her mother had never liked her to. She had never had any sympathy with her mother's fears in the past. She watched the swift passage of the water as Indian Charlie pulled upstream to the float, aware of the complete hopelessness of any search, and hearing over and over again Pete's impatient words, "There wasn't any other."

"No other boy," said Sara McDermott to herself. "Then this one, like the one at the pool, not a real boy, but a messenger. What is it the French say? A *revenant, one returned*—Johnny—and I should have lost him now, if I hadn't lost him then. I should be standing here now, with Pete telling me that my John is drowned."

It was not until she heard Pete explaining to Charlie that he should go with her to call on Mrs. Bettenger that she realized that something was required of her, and that it would be more difficult than anything she had yet faced in her life. To approach a stranger and tell her that her son, her John—what was the lost boy's name?— was drowned.

Charlie climbed out of his boat, which, released, swung downstream with rapidity and hung there, pulling at its painter. He walked "stumpy," as John had said. He was as short as she was, and thick. His face was weathered, and the lower part of it covered with a white stubble, but his deep-set blue eyes, under the shaggy, sandy brows, were comprehending.

"Well, Missus," he said, "it seems we're the only ones as can go see her now. So we must."

"Of course we must, Charlie," she said, and together they walked off toward the old house. The path was sandy, worn into the grass. Pink mallows were in blossom beside it in scattered clumps. It forked, as it neared the fence, and a new path ran from the old one toward the rail fence. The old path, a little farther on, had gone down, undermined by the river, into the sandy cove below. They climbed the fence.

"What was the boy's name, Charlie?" she asked as they drew near the thick old lilac bushes by the porch.

"I don't rightly know," he had answered when someone unseen came out on the porch and called:

"Bill-ee, oh, Bill."

A woman met them as they rounded the lilacs.

"We won't have to tell her," thought Sara suddenly. "She'll know by our faces."

But Charlie had taken off his hat and was saying what had to be said.

"Mrs. Bettenger, we got bad news for you."

All her life Sara thought she would remember the dignity of that speech and be grateful to Indian Charlie for having taken the responsibility of it upon himself.

She was not prepared for the fierce vitality with which this woman met their account of the event. She wanted to rush to the river. Sara was afraid she would want to plunge into it and search the bottom with her hands. They could not explain to her that it was useless to search, that nets and grappling irons would be useless, that the child's body must be swept down-channel by now. They agreed to phone from the Point for help, for every kind of searcher, but it would be too late. It was already too late. Finally she became convinced, and wept violently, hysterically. Charlie, over her bowed head, for they had persuaded her, half by force, to be seated on the rattan bench on the veranda, said to Sara McDermott:

"I'll be going to Dr. Reid. You stay with her. We'll be back as fast as I can find him."

Sara saw him go, stumping down the path, feeling that a mighty moral support was being withdrawn with him. The mother of the drowned boy lifted her head, when they were alone, and turned upon her with bitterness.

"It's all very well for you to stand there and try to say comforting things to me—you, with no children. Oh yes, I know who you are. I've heard about your family from the Hudsons. You can't understand. You've never had a child. You couldn't bear to stand there at all if you had ever had a child." She broke off her tirade abruptly and fell again to violent weeping.

Sara, looking down upon her, made no attempt to defend herself against the charge of complete childlessness. Strangely enough, she felt no bitterness and no resentment at this woman's bitterness. She had entered into a state of inner calmness. She had seen John.

She remembered the unqualified loneliness which she had felt after the birth, and death, of her son. She had felt then as if she had been the only woman in the world who had suffered thus. She saw no reason why she should have been treated so by fate. She had done everything she could to make it a safe birth. It had been taken out of her hands by circumstances which no one could have prevented or foreseen, not even the most skilled of physicians. There had been no one to blame. It had simply happened, and she had been left alone with her loss. That loneliness had not lasted, however. Some way or other it had disappeared, had melted. What was the phrase that her mother's colored laundress had used? She had been washing clothes for her mother, and talk-

ing about her troubles. Her arms deep in the suds in the
old stationary tub, Irene had turned her head to say, in
her slow, soft voice, "But somehow or other, they gets
gone. The grace of the Lord just eats 'em away."

Like the spring warmth eating away the ice at the
edge of the river, Sara had thought then. Now she
thought that was what had happened to her first loneliness. The grace of the Lord had eaten it away, like ice
in the river. And after Judy's sorrow she had understood
that other women lost their children too, and that it
could be a bond of deep affection between them.

She did not try to argue with Mrs. Bettenger. She
waited; waited until Charlie Stuart returned with Dr.
Reid, and until Dr. Reid had managed to get a hypo-
dermic into Mrs. Bettenger's arm. Then she led her
into the house and put her to bed, filled a hot-water
bottle and put it to her feet, piled blankets above her
shaking, exhausted body. After a time the patient fell
asleep. Sara knew that Dr. Reid had taken charge of such
messages as must be sent from the Point, which had the
only telephone on the island. She knew that the lost
boy's father would arrive in a few days, and that Dr.
Reid would come back that evening. She sat down by
the kitchen table and leaned her head on her hands.

Perhaps in the succeeding days she would find out
who the fair-headed boy had been. Perhaps she would
see him again. It did not matter much, at that moment.
She had seen John, according to the illumination of her
own heart. She knew that he was always alive for her.
She knew that he had drawn her closer to Judy, and, in
her inarticulate sympathy, closer to the woman asleep
in the next room. It did not matter then whether Mrs.

Bettenger ever realized the bitterness of her attack upon this woman who had wanted to help her, or whether she ever became her friend. She understood Mrs. Bettenger, and was sorry for her, and could help her, humbly, in simple, earthly ways. In a few days the boy's father would be here and take over. In a few days Judy and the children would be here. What a beginning of the summer for them all! She would not let it cloud the summer for them if she could help it. The children should swim in the river, but not at this beach. The river, impersonal, beneficent, and destructive without choice, should be for Judy's children the source of joy which it had always been for Sara as a child. Sara herself would see its beauty again, like the beauty of an archangel, resplendent with light.

The evening before her cousin's arrival at the island Sara McDermott wrote a long letter to her husband in which she described her meeting with the boy in the poplar wood, and all the details of the few hours following her visit with the boy. Then she read it over and tore it up. Her belief in the supernatural quality of the boy seemed too unfounded, set down in simple words. She could not express the fringes of perception, the sudden, unsummoned emotion concerning him. She felt that Tom would think she was losing her grip, that coming to reopen the cottage by herself had been too much for her, whereas the truth was that the earlier part of the day on which the tragedy had occurred had been one of the happiest she could remember, and that she had never felt saner or more reconciled to the fate which had been portioned out to her than she had on that sunny, very busy morning. She wrote another letter, telling him what had occurred, but without mentioning the boy in the wood, and promised herself that when he came she would tell him about it all. It would be much easier to talk about it than to write it. Tom would set her straight, bring her back to the level path of reason, as he had done before. And as she considered this, as before, she was not entirely sure that she wanted to be brought back to reason or talked out of her ghost. In the end, when Tom did come for his few weeks with her and Judy and the three young cousins, they were all too busy for many long, quiet conversations, and Sara did not mention her ideas about those who return from the dead. She told herself that there had been nothing unnatural or impossible about the meeting, and that she no longer suspected herself of "seeing ghosts in broad daylight," but the ultimate truth was that she wanted to leave that visit untouched, unspoken of, unblurred.

The depression which began that autumn did things to the cabin-cruiser business. After a year of working against the inevitable Tom's firm closed down, and Tom came back to Chicago, looking for another job. He formed some connections at Gary with the Great Lakes shipping, picked up some advisory, semigovernmental work, and managed to keep going, still as a marine architect. He spent some time in Detroit, more in Chicago, and Sara returned to Kensington, not to the house which they had formerly occupied, but to another, not too far from Judy's. There was plenty to do. Interest in the League of Women Voters led to her presence on the Kensington City Council, and she gave that up to run a cafeteria for the Kensington High School. The shipbuilding business pulled itself together again slowly.

The number of freighters on the Great Lakes increased.
By 1936 Tom was having all the work to do that he
could handle, and Sara was wondering if she ought not
to give up the cafeteria in order to help him more. She
did not want to. She liked feeding the young ones, and
she liked the social contacts which belonged to the job.
The first summer which Judy and the children had spent
at the island with her had been so successful that they
had repeated it every year. Through the first years of the
thirties they had fared very simply, but the island had
been the best place in the world to relearn the simple
life. Judy's boys had supplied the table with fish—in
those years even pike had been acceptable. It had cut
the meat bill way down and had given the boys a great
sense of accomplishment.

Sara was thinking of this on the June morning in 1936
when the third visit of her ghost took place. It was a hot
morning, as hot and sticky as Illinois can be in late June,
and the house was in confusion, for Sara was packing to
go north. School was out, the cafeteria closed. Sara, in a
crumpled linen dress, the sleeves pushed back above the
elbows, was emptying closets, brushing woolens and
packing them away in mothballs. Pausing in the lower
hallway on one of her trips from attic to cellar, she
noticed that the candles were still in the seven-branched
candlestick, and stopped to remove them, laying them
straight on the bare cool marble top of the table, for they
already felt soft. Last year she had forgotten the candles,
and, reopening the house on a fairly cool September day,
she had been greeted by a candelabrum from which the
candles leaned in a complete salaam, the result of some
warm August afternoon. She was not entirely happy.

Although she looked forward to the coolness of the island, and the sight of Judy's children running barefoot down the twisting paths, she disliked the prospect of leaving Tom in rooms in the city. He had decided that he could not spare much time for a vacation, and he would be more comfortable in town than in a house without a housekeeper. She heard someone coming up the brick walk and went on with what she was doing until she heard a light rap on the screen door. A boy was there, in silhouette against the light.

He was selling magazines, a boy of about sixteen, and he looked so hot that she asked him to come in, although she did not want to buy any of his publications. He seemed to know her, but that was not surprising. Almost all the high school children knew her.

He followed her into the shadowy living room, tossed his magazines on a table, and collapsed into a low armchair. He did not really collapse, but the way in which he sat down and stretched out his legs before him suggested the most complete relaxation.

"Coolest place I've been today," he said in great enjoyment.

"Not very cool at that," said Sara, aware of the heat descending upon the green awnings.

The boy looked about the room appraisingly, and Sara saw his attention caught by the model of a full-rigged clipper ship on the mantel of the empty fireplace.

"Nice thing that," he said, sitting up straight to look at it better. "Veree, veree nice." He was not tall, but well built, and well proportioned, rather slight, in spite of the squareness of his shoulders.

"He's been growing fast," thought Sara, "and hasn't

yet caught up with his bones. What a lot he looks like Tom!" But nothing startled her, nothing warned her that the resemblance might be more than accidental.

She said jokingly, "Working your way through college?"

"Oh, not yet," he answered. "I'm on trial. They told me that if I made a good enough showing this week they'd take me on as a regular salesman. But it's all a racket. Just a way to get a week's work out of you free. I can't sell that stuff. My heart isn't in it." He laughed. "I'm going to clear out this afternoon and get me a real job across the lake."

"What do you mean, a real job?" said Sara.

"Working on a farm. I'm going across to Michigan. They always have work for a handy man, pitching hay or something. And they give you good eats on a farm. I can work my way north."

"That does sound more like something," she agreed.

"Oh, definitely," he answered in the latest high school manner. "I should stay in the city all summer! I'd suffocate. There's an excursion steamer leaving this afternoon for Ludington. I can bum a ride over, I'm certain— cabin boy or something. Dishwasher, maybe. They do wash dishes on boats, don't they? Then I can hike upstate, working as I go."

"You've got it all figured out, haven't you?" said Sara. Her heart warmed to his enthusiasm, and she began to feel herself more in the mood for starting on a journey.

"Well, but definitely," said he. "Worked it out this morning, on the burning pavements of Kensington, and me not selling anything. I saw the announcement of the sailing of the *Westland* down at the station, and the idea come to me all at once, like that."

"Where does she sail from, and when?"

"Chicago River, you know, same place the *Manitou* and the *Missouri* used to dock. At two-thirty. I can make it into town nicely. Plenty of time if I hitchhike. Don't you think it's a good idea?"

"Why, yes," said Sara slowly. "It sounds like fun."

"I think I owe myself a summer like that. Footloose, you know. Have to go to the university in the fall. I may not get another chance to be a hobo for quite a while."

The room was so shadowy that she could not make out the color of his eyes; they seemed dark, but they might have been blue. The voice had begun to touch at some memory—she could not quite place it. But how likable he was! He made her feel refreshed by his very eagerness.

"A fellow has got to get off on his own once in a while, you know," he said.

"Surely," she answered. "I agree with you. It sounds fine. I'd like to do it myself, if I could."

"Well," he said, looking toward his magazines, "I'd better begin to ramble."

"You can leave me a couple of those," she said, weakening, and excusing herself by the thought that they'd be nice to read on the train the next day. "I'll get you some money. How would you like a glass of cold buttermilk before you start?"

"I'd like it fine," he said, rising when she did.

"Sit down again, then, and I'll be back in a minute," she said, and left him standing in front of the fireplace, inspecting more closely the model of the *Ariel*.

When she returned, with the glass in her hand, he was gone. The magazines were gone too; he had not left any for her. Nothing else was touched. It struck her at first as amazingly unmannered of him. He must have been afraid of not catching his boat, and thought he couldn't spare another minute, even for cold buttermilk. Then she realized that the explanation was entirely out of character for him. He had been casual but perfectly courteous. Even upon such short acquaintance she was certain that he would never have been rude in just that fashion. Something must have called him away.

She stepped to the door, looking across the elm-shaded lawn to the vacant street. There was no one in sight. She had not been in the kitchen very long; she had not yet taken time to look for change for the magazines. How could he have disappeared so swiftly?

She returned to the living room, where she had last seen him standing before the mantel, looking at the ship, and as the image of him returned fully to her mind's eyes she knew who he was. The premonition of disaster was swift in descending.

She had been warned, but was it for his sake or the sake of another? If she had been quick enough, the last time, she might have prevented the tragedy. What could she do now? In what direction would the lightning strike? She stood, her hand clutching the long portiere at the doorway of the living room, in such a panic of apprehension that she could not pull her wits together. She began to relive the visit, slowly and painfully, from the moment when she had laid the last candle on the table top and gone to open the screen door. She went through the conversation step by step. The *Westland*, she thought. When have I heard the *Westland* spoken of lately? Wasn't that the ship which Tom had been called in about, last winter? He had been asked to inspect some old vessel, an old cargo ship remodeled as a passenger boat, which was to be put in use as an excursion steamer. He had looked it over and declared it unfit for such a use unless the system of ballast were remodeled. Wasn't that the ship? She had not paid much attention at the time. His theory had been that, with the new superstructure, the promenade decks, and no heavy cargo in the hold, the boat would be topheavy. It had been a routine sort of examination. He had turned in his report and had not mentioned the subject again. That was it. The boy had made such a point of it—the *Westland,* sailing from such and such a pier at two-thirty. What time was it now? He had been telling her as plainly as he could. He had come to her because Tom must know. It all came perfectly clear in her mind as soon as she remembered the name. She went to the phone and called Tom's office.

"Tom," she said as soon as she heard his voice, "that old boat, the *Westland,* the one you said wasn't safe, it's going to sail this afternoon at two-thirty. You'll have to stop it."

There was a short pause, as if he were trying to shift his attention from one subject to another. Then his voice:

"The *Westland?* Oh yeah. It was unsafe as I found it. I recommended certain changes. They must have fixed it up or it wouldn't be in service. What's hit you, Sary? You sound all het up."

"Well, if you think it's safe . . ." she answered. "I

just had it awfully firm in my mind that it had been condemned. Then I heard it was going to sail. It rather gave me a fright."

"They asked me to look it over," said Tom. "They would hardly have done that if they hadn't meant to do something about it. They didn't report to me about any changes, but I gave 'em detailed instructions. It must be all right. By the way, I ordered that outboard motor for the *Bean-boat*. You ought to be getting it at the island in a week or two."

"Thank you," she said. "You're a lamb. It will make the children happy."

She hung up and returned to the front part of the house. There was the glass of buttermilk still on the table in the hall. She had not told Tom about the boy. If she had, and if she had been able to convey her sense of a supernatural warning, would he have taken her alarm more seriously? Tom was so sane that the very thought of him was like a steadying hand.

"Careful, my girl," she said to herself. "Take it easy. There was a boy, all right, but the town is full of boys." And then, "But why did he run off without his buttermilk?" The answer came, half whimsical, half terrifying: "Of course, *a ghost can't eat*."

What time was it? She was not wearing her wrist watch. She ran upstairs to find it and was astonished to see the hands pointing at five minutes to one. "I thought it was nearer noon," she said. "Have I been in a daze? The boy thought he had plenty of time to make the boat. Surely it was still before noon when he came."

"Plenty of time to hitchhike," he had said, and at that sudden vivid recollection of him, she abandoned all attempt to deny him for her own or to avoid his message. She hurried downstairs again to the phone and put in a call for Tom's office. And waited.

She could hear the phone ringing again, and then again. Why didn't he answer it? It was right there on his desk, within easy reach of his hand. It rang again, far away in an endless distance of humming sound. Finally she heard the receiver lifted. A woman's voice answered. Sara asked for Tom.

"Sorry," said the light, faraway voice, "he's just gone out, about five minutes ago. Any message?"

"His wife called," said Sara, and hung up.

She stood looking out the window at the deep noon shadows on the hot lawn. "He might be gone for lunch. He can't be coming home—he said he'd be late tonight. I can't do anything without him. I can't stop a boat from sailing without some authority. Dear Father in heaven, what shall I do?"

The long drive to the city absorbed her attention somewhat, although as she drove she was tormented by two emotions: the sense of apprehension, which she could not shake off, and the fear of not being able to make a comprehensible explanation to Tom. She regretted now that she had not tried to tell him about the boy in the poplar wood. It was two o'clock before she reached the Loop, and the traffic was bad, as bad as it ever could be on a Saturday afternoon. She drove around and around the block in which Tom's office building stood, looking for a place to park the car, her anguish of apprehension growing with every minute which delayed her. She had to leave the car and go all the way to the fourteenth floor, hoping against hope that Tom would have returned to the office since she called. She had no doubt but that he would come with her, at her appeal; how she was to rationalize herself to him did not matter as much as finding him and taking him back to the car.

He had returned, and he went with her without a murmur. On the way down in the elevator he said, "You got me rather worried, Sary, so I hopped over to the office of the commission to see what I could find out. I couldn't raise 'em by phone, and when I got there I found everything buttoned up tight. So I don't know what's been done about the old tub. I can't believe they'd be so careless as to let her into the excursion service without an overhauling, though."

In the street he looked at her curiously and remarked, "Sure the heat hasn't been getting you down? You don't usually worry about hunches."

"It *is* a hunch," she admitted, "not the heat," and as they drove toward the river, under the broken black shadow of the elevated, past the crowding trucks, in the curious suffocating odor of roasting coffee and gasoline fumes, she tried to tell him about her boy in the poplar wood, the brief, enchanted visit, of the boy in the shadows of the living room that morning, and of how they were both the little boy at the pool with the turtle in his hand. Tom, who was driving, glanced at her now and then, neither believing nor disbelieving, as far as she could make out, but serious and interested. When she had said her last word he kept silent for a minute or two and then summed it up according to his own decision.

"I don't know about your ghost, Sary, but I do know

that the *Westland* is a topheavy old tub, and I think they
might have had the decency to report to me about her
before loading her up with a Saturday excursion crowd."

They did not reach the pier. Before they were within
a block of it they found the street roped off and a policeman in charge. The *Westland*, unballasted, crowded
with passengers, had simply rolled over at the pier, when
most of her passengers had rushed to the farther deck to
see a flight of planes, and had filled the Chicago River
with drowning men and women.

It had taken Sara McDermott a long time before she
could put that experience away, before she could say
of it, to Tom, a coincidence, an astonishing coincidence,
but still something within the bounds of what was considered possible experience. She had never thought of
herself as psychic, and she did not do so after this. She
was a deeply religious person, who belonged to no codified
religion. Her life was all outward-going, practical and
active, and she was haunted by no other memories. On
that December evening in 1941, when she had returned
from giving a soldier a lift to San Jose, she went to bed,
and slept, but in her sleep, and in her waking moments
between dreams, she remembered all the times when
she had seen a boy who seemed to be her son.

The Sunday morning was clear and mild. Sara woke to
an expectation and a fear which was there before her
almost the moment she opened her eyes. She did not feel
nervous, or tired, physically, but she did feel involved
in a slow and abiding emotion, a sense of waiting. By
daylight the situation was just as strange and just as
incomprehensible as it had been at dusk.

After the sinking of the *Westland* she had searched

the lists of the drowned and of the survivors for the name
of a boy from Kensington or from some nearby suburb,
but had found none. As Tom had pointed out to her,
it was quite possible that the boy had been turned from
his plan at the last minute. Perhaps he had not had time
for the trip from the city; perhaps his family had objected. Tom had quite naturally provided him with a
family, another family, not the McDermotts. The fact
that Sara had heard the *Westland* discussed as unsafe
had probably been dormant in her mind through the
half year or so preceding the announcement that it was
about to be put into service again. It had been there, a
fear, and had risen to join with this old desire of hers, to
see her boy again as he would have looked had he lived
to be sixteen years old. And as for the lad's speaking
to her as if he knew her, why, every child in Kensington
High School knew her. She was, for that generation of
Kensingtonians, as famous as the principal. All this was
true, she admitted as she went about the morning routine,
and yet the suspended emotion was there, and was as
much a fact as any other part of her experience. There
was also the recent memory of the face of a fair young
man under the small khaki cap. She did not wish to turn
away from that memory. She even doubted whether it
was morally right to do so. Why should she try to deny
the meaning which he had for her, any more than she
should try to deny, to shut her eyes to the perpetual
mystery of life, and of death?

The letter for Tom was still to be mailed. She drove
into the nearest village to mail it, and all the way in, as
the road wound between the low hills, and the early sunlight lay fresh upon the empty orchards, the fields with

their first covering of green, the sense of news to be brought to her was sharp in her mind. So sharp was this sense that, after she had posted the letter, the first person she spoke to seemed to be approaching her with an announcement. But it was only the customary greeting from a neighbor on his way to the drugstore for a paper, and what had seemed an especial interest in his face had only been a surprise at seeing her in town so early on a Sunday.

"Everything all right up at the ranch, Mrs. McDermott?"

"Everything all right, thanks."

"Fine day for this time of year."

"Fine day," she had agreed, and walked across the bright, empty street to her car.

Returned to the house, she scanned the morning paper for news of an accident involving a young flier. There had been such items, too many of them. A soldier killed at a railroad crossing near Fort Ord. The crash of a training plane in Oklahoma. Collision of a bus and a vegetable truck in the hills outside Monterey. She had seen similar items, noted briefly, seldom on the first page, too many times before, but this morning nothing of the sort met her eye. She laid the paper down and went into the kitchen to wash the dishes. She waited for the phone to ring. She thought, "Perhaps whatever it was happened too early this morning to make the papers." She swept the kitchen, made her bed, and returned to the front room, where she switched on the radio for a little music to fill the expectant silence.

She had no feeling that she must do anything to prevent what might be coming. She felt, indeed, that there was nothing she could do. Twice before she had thought she could prevent the tragedy which impended. This time it seemed to her only that she must wait. She would work in the garden. Outdoors she would feel less the emptiness of the house, Tom's absence, and the weight of something to come. She had forgotten to buy the ranunculus bulbs after all, but there was plenty else to do. She stood at the front door, looking across the terrace to her neighbor's orchard, the small trees hazy with light, leafless, but shimmering with the haze of twigs, sloping in peaceful files where the ground dipped before rising to the mountains, and she thought, "Perhaps no bad news is coming after all. Perhaps the day will go by serenely, unmarred, as tranquil as this view that I have grown to love so much. Perhaps I really am just the silly fool that Tom would have every right to think me—and I hope I am. But if this thing I'm waiting for does come, this sorrow for some woman I don't even know the name of," she thought, with a sudden decision, "then I'll know, I'll know for myself beyond a doubt that I've seen my boy."

The earth would be soft and easy to work. It exhaled an autumn sweetness of dead leaves and of violets, under the protection of the thorny blackberry bushes. She would go, in just a moment, and fetch the trowel and her garden gloves. She was about to turn off the radio, but the song which was on the air at that moment was in French, and she liked it. She waited for it to be finished, standing in the sunlit doorway, her eyes on the files of shimmering trees, and so heard the announcement which interrupted the song.

"Our naval base at Pearl Harbor has been attacked by Japanese planes."

So that was it. Curious, she had not expected it to come over the radio. She had been waiting for some smaller, more personal event. But this—this touched them all.

She knew now, beyond all question, unshakably. She knew that John had been a true messenger. She knew also that this was the last time she would have lost him, and that this time, as at all the other times, except the very first, she would not have been alone. Neither would these other women be alone. Was that a comfort? she asked herself, and answered, slowly and honestly, that she believed it was, the greatest possible. It was not that she wished grief to be multiplied and extended, but that it might be shared, and that the weight of it might thus be made less. Her sense of kinship with Judy, not only in Judy's grief but in her happiness in the three other children, had been the deeper because of the small boy at the pool. Through all these years the boy in the poplar wood, the boy in the shadowy living room at Kensington, looking at the model *Ariel*, had drawn her closer to other women, in joy as well as in sorrow. She had never lost him.

"You never lose a person whom you have truly loved," said Sara McDermott, with her eyes on the rain-washed hills, the winter-quiet orchard.

The Breakable Cup

~~~~~~

Illinois 1905

M AGGIE WAS his friend, not his enemy. He knew that well, and yet he stepped outside into the late summer afternoon with insults ringing in his small head—admonitions, recriminations and insults. And whether deserved or not, he was hurt, and he was alone.

He had been clumsy and destructive. He had not meant to be destructive. As for the clumsiness, he was too young to plead his own case, even to himself. Standing before a table, even with his chin lifted and his neck stretched, he did not have much of a view of what was on it. The same with Maggie's dresser.

"Put this on my dresser," she had said in her sweetest voice, indicating with her bare elbow the satin-padded box, holding her flour-dusted hands before her, wanting to get on with her baking, not wanting to pause to wash and dry her hands before touching her treasure. The box was covered with blue satin, hand-painted with forget-me-nots and violets and small roses. He admired it, too. He did not stop to reason that Maggie, hasty as usual, had not thought to put the box away herself, before coming with the mixing bowl to the kitchen table.

"Are your own hands clean now?" she had thought to inquire, and, since they were, he took the precious box, and, in Maggie's bedroom, which was entered from the kitchen, he placed the box on the dresser top, gave it a gentle but determined push away from the edge, and heard a glass topple upon the marble with a swish of falling leaves and flowers. And then he knew that he had knocked over the vase of posies that Maggie kept before the photograph of her young man.

A trickle of water reached the edge of the marble. He could not see whether it attained the box. Maggie was in the doorway before he could either report the disaster or escape. She lifted her apron and wrapped it about the box, and then, with the water still dripping audibly behind her, and the box clasped to her middle, her face flushed, her eyes wide with indignation, she had delivered her insults. Like all grown people, she had everything on her side—reason, power, and great resources of language. At five—if he was as old as five at that time—he did not go to school yet—he had only his sense of good intention, and his small, derided dignity.

A middle-western summer surrounded the town. Even at five—and when he remembered the day over the long stretch of years, he could not be sure that he was even five—he was well aware of the town as a town, with a center, and with defined edges. It was surrounded by fields, terminated at one side by the

Saint Charles River. Beyond the river, where back yards sloped down to docks and boat-houses, there were fields, patches of oak woods, dirt roads lined by burdock and goldenrod. He had walked with Maggie to the edge of the town and across the bridge, to get buttermilk. The town had always been there. The houses were settled into the earth, with cool cellars, and sloping cellar doors over flights of cool steps leading down into the earth. The prairie grass grew close up against the foundations. The oak trees over-hung the roofs, the elms swung their branches close to the second-storey windows, all as if the trees and the houses had been co-eval. And yet he knew that at one time Indians had lived here. There had been bark lodges on the banks of the river, and he himself had in his possession a flint arrow-head which an elder had one day placed in his hand. There were also the trail-marking trees, thick trees bent double to the ground, which had been bent when they were young by Indians. As far as he was concerned, they had al-ways been stout trees, bent to the ground. In other words, he had very little sense of time. He would rather have liked to meet an Indian. He did not know that he had already passed a good many Indians on the main street of the town. They had not carried bows and arrows.

He stood, then, just outside the back door, framed in its beds of golden-glow, chiefly aware of his soli-tude and the assault on his dignity. But the afternoon itself was not to be ignored, the haze, the brooding warmth. The kitchen garden lay before him beyond a short stretch of untended lawn. Pieplant, whose big leaves stood higher than his knees, rose from the crumbling, sun-faded earth. The thick juicy stems would be warm to touch and sour to taste. He went on, avoiding the harsh and hairy leaves of the squash plants. By the tomatoes he stopped, and crouched. He had given himself an occupation; he was looking for caterpillars. But his problem with Maggie remained uppermost in his mind. She was not his enemy. She was his friend, and for that his disgrace rankled the more.

He had seen the photograph of the young man before whom she had set the flowers. She had lifted it down for him to consider. She was going to be married to him some day; she would go back to Ireland then.

"Sure we could be married the day his old mother would die," she said. "He has to stay and care for her. She's an old, old woman. Sure she has the right to die. She keeps the young from having any life of their own."

She talked like that, did Maggie, and her voice and words were different from the talk of other people. Her room was different from the other rooms in the house. It had a different smell, and different treasures. There was a crucifix hung on the wall by her bed. She talked to him about leprechauns. She had said, even, that she knew an old man who had seen a leprechaun.

He knew that his mother paid her five dollars a week, and was training her. At the end of a year she would leave them for a place with more money. But a year was forever; and meanwhile she had grown into

his life. By and by on this same afternoon she would
come in search of him. She would give him a hug,
and she would doubtless have baked something good
to eat. Gingerbread perhaps. He was clumsy; he admitted it. He dropped things. Cups and glasses had a
way of tipping over when he was near them.

Maggie had no friends in the town, as yet. His
mother had said to her, "Maggie, wouldn't you like
to go to the movies some night?" Maggie had replied,
"Oh, no, Missis. There you'd see every kind of bad
parable. The Father advises against it." This was not
his father she spoke of; this was a priest. He had not
seen a priest, that he could remember.

His eyes searched the vines, the tangled green
stems with their faint fur of white, their ragged
leaves. He was aware of the strong odor of the plants,
and of the small green fruit, the larger green fruit
turning red, and the amazing round red forms which
appeared so splendidly in all this dull tangle and
confusion, but his profounder attention was strug-
gling with the question of why Maggie, who was a
good girl—he was sure of that—was wishing for an
old woman to die, Maggie was not old, of course. She
was grown-up. His mother, who was more grown-up
than Maggie, was not old either. There was no old
person living in his home. He had seen old women in
the distance, in other gardens, walking slowly toward back doors, bent, and uncertain of their move-
ments, dressed sadly in dark colors. They were to be
avoided. And in the postoffice with his mother, waiting for the mail to be sorted, he had seen an old man
who sat behind the stove, with a cane, and with his

head on his hands on the crook of the cane. The face was yellowish, the chin and the cheeks covered with greyish stubble. There was moisture on the wrinkled skin about the corners of the eyes, and sometimes the old man wiped his nose with the back of his hand. He was rather afraid of the old man. Perhaps he merely disliked him. In any case, he wished the old man were not there. "Sure he has the right to die," he thought. "Why does he sit around in the postoffice, being unpleasant?"

His mother had gone off hours ago, before lunch time, wearing a pink dimity dress which he liked. It had a sash of black satin with a long fringe. She wore a black straw hat high on her head. Before she picked up the hat from the bed he had admired the pink roses on it. When she wore it he could not see the roses, but he knew they were there, and he was pleased with her for wearing the dress with the soft stuff that flowed down to her ankles. She went off on foot to the other end of town to have lunch with friends. She ought to come home soon. She would, perhaps, bring him a flat pink peppermint or some other trifle to show that she had not forgotten him. Well, after Labor Day he would go to school, and he would take his lunch in a tin box, like his father, and then he would be independent of them all, and have friends of his own. Meanwhile he searched the tomatoe vines, lifting a leaf, now and then, cautiously, and presently he found what he was looking for. He did not disturb it; he merely looked at it.

It was enormously fat, bulging in regular segments, smooth, pale green, decorated with gold dots,

and with tufts of white bristles. At its rear end it had a
horn something like a rosethorn, curved and reddish,
extremely elegant. At the other end it had a mouth,
no doubt about that, but he could not see that it had
either teeth or tushes. It was great. It was at once both
terrifying and beautiful. It was more beautiful than
fearsome, for him. He gloated over it, and his delight
was so great that he did not hear Maggie's approach
until she was practically upon him.

"You couldn't answer now could you, you leprechaun," she said, "down on your hunkers hiding
from Maggie behind a tomatoe bush. I called you
three times. Your mother phoned. She's not to be
home until late. Dust the clods off your knees. Come
into the house now." They proceeded toward the
house, Maggie behind him as if he might try to run
away. "Your mother, she was to take tea this afternoon with the old woman in the big house with the
iron railing. So now she can't do that. But she left a
jar of jelly on the hall table, and you're to take that,
and you're to explain to the old woman that circumstances beyond her control are interfering with her
keeping the engagement. Though why your mother'd
trust you with a thing like that is more than I can
understand. But one thing I know, you'll have to be
cleaner than you are the now."

When he was cleaner, and Maggie had brushed his
hair, which had a way of falling almost into his eyes
when it was not slicked back with water, he walked
down the street toward the house with the iron rail-
ings. It was not far. In after years he seemed to arrive
at it in a few steps. It seemed far to him on this day.

He walked slowly, carrying the jar in both hands, naturally, because neither hand alone could have encompassed it, and he walked slowly because the sidewalk was uneven, and it would have been the easiest thing in the world to stub a toe, and be thrown off-balance. Then he would need both hands to save his neck, and what would become of the jelly! His mother had wrapped it in white tissue paper and tied a pink ribbon about it. It looked for all the world like a birthday present. A conviction grew on him that it was a birthday present.

The street was the next thing to being deserted. Once an automobile passed him, holding to the middle of the road where the dirt had been oiled; and once the bright green delivery wagon of Nisson's the Grocer rolled briskly by, the horse stepping along at a lively rate, very different from the horses that pulled the ice-wagon or the milk-wagon. There were no children. Children with whom he sometimes played had a way of disappearing from his world without warning or explanation. Sometimes they came back, and said they had been on a visit. Their mothers had taken them to see an aunt or a grandmother, or even just to look at some scenery. Like himself, they moved without individual volition in the wake of their elders, making what observations and friendships they could, hailing each other in a sandpile one afternoon, then never meeting again; visiting with people who had time for them—like Maggie, in her good moments. Like a youngish woman who sat on the steps of her sideporch a few houses away, drying her hair one morning. He had quite a good talk with this woman. What had he been doing that day? Ah, yes, he had been picking dandelions up and down the street, and she had been there, shaking her hair in the June sunlight. He had walked by the house dawdling hopefully a number of times since. He had not seen her again.

Beneath his feet the slate, flaked in curious patterns, variants of circles and ellipses, shone like rainwater. The slabs tilted this way and that, shadowed by elm trees, specked sometimes with twigs or leaves; the first faintly yellowing leaves of that approaching September when he would go to school. Presently, to one side of the walk appeared the stone foundation for the iron fence.

The gate, fortunately, was easy to unlatch. He did it with his right hand, holding the jar firmly against his stomach with the other, and he went up a stone step, and then another, to the smooth stone walk to the house, feeling elated. In spite of Maggie's jibes about the probable fate of the jelly, he was doing very well. He was entrusted with a mission, after all. His mother knew he was dependable. And it was an adventure to pass beyond the iron railing into a yard which he had entered only once before, and about which he had many speculations. He had never been inside the house. He had stood on the doorstep once with his mother while she had delivered a bunch of flowers and made some inquiries. Someone must have been ill. Yes, that was it. Someone had been ill, and you did not enter a house where someone was ill unless you were a doctor or a nurse.

The steps to the porch were a shade less high than

he had remembered. But the bell was not easy to reach. It was set in the middle of the door, and you turned it, as if you were winding up a toy. He heard it ring as in a remote distance.

While he waited for the footsteps which followed on the ring he looked back down the stone walk and across the smooth lawn to the street. There were enormous bushes on either side of the doorstep. They were extraordinarily symmetrical, with little fine dark green leaves presenting a surface like plush. The lawn looked as if someone had brushed it. It swept around the house, sloping slightly, and away under the trees and past masses of shrubbery, as if it were not in a town at all, but in a park, and might end only at the river. It would be great if, his errand accomplished, he need not return to the street, but could follow the dip of the land into all that space and mystery. He held the jelly firmly in both hands and waited.

"My mother will be disappointed," said the woman to whom he handed the jelly, and gave his message, when the door was opened.

He nodded gravely as if he understood everything, which was far from the truth, and he turned to step down. The thought that he might ask permission to explore the yard occurred to him and was dismissed, very rapidly, as he stood poised. He would prefer to explore, if at all, without permission. To ask permission would be too much like exposing a secret. But as he stood, about to leave, the woman said firmly, "You must just stay and be a guest in place of your mother," and he found himself almost immediately in the entrance hall, the door closing behind him.

He lifted his short little nose and sniffed the air, instinctively. What had he got into? The air was confined, not stuffy, but an indoors air, unmoving and weighted with unfamiliar scents. Wax, spice, dried flowers? He could not unravel it. He took a good look now at his hostess. She was definitely old, according to his ideas, but by no means unpleasant. Grey hair, a shortish figure, a plain dress that might have been blue or grey in the half-light of the hall. Her mother must be very old. He hazarded an inquiry.

"Is it your mother's birthday?"

"No. No one's birthday. Though I may say she has had a great many birthdays, first and last. Would you come to her next birthday party? She will be ninety. We should have a party. Thank you for reminding me of it. She's my husband's mother, really; not mine, except by courtesy."

"I see," he said politely, not understanding much except that word ninety, which was as good as a hundred. Was the mother of Maggie's young man a hundred years old, he wondered? Then he said with formality, as he had observed people speaking at church, "I suppose she's really your grandmother."

"No," said his hostess. "She's my husband's mother. He has been gone a long time—dear me, a very long time. And of course his father died even longer ago. We live here together. Two old women in a big house. So you see, it is a disappointment that your mother could not come. But my mother will be very pleased to see you. She likes young people. Wait here a moment. No, wait in the sun porch."

She guided him down the hallway, past an étagère of dark wood, with mirrors and many ornaments. The wood shone with little glints, the mirrors reflected shadows. He had a sense of a stairway going up into further shadows, and of large rooms passed by. Then he found himself in a small bright room full of plants and wicker furniture.

"Sit here," said his hostess, indicating a chair, and left him.

He was painfully obedient. From the chair he could not see very well through the large windows which filled three sides of the room, but he felt that he was now at the back of the house. If he could get a good look through the windows he would know whether the lawn ran down to the water, whether there was a stable, a boathouse. His curiosity and his sense of responsibility lifted him. He felt that it would be fearsome to meet a person who was ninety years old. On the other hand, he already felt a distinct liking for the old woman who was his hostess, and he must not let his mother down, his own mother, who, from where he sat in this house of old women, appeared most delightfully young.

On a table quite near him, spread with a white cloth, there were things for tea—a tea-pot, very tall, and an enormous sugar-bowl with a lid, flowers in a vase, dishes with little cakes, some flashes of silver, or burnished copper, and three cups, each on a saucer. Such cups he had never seen before. His spirits continued to rise. He forgot that he was the most clumsy spalpeen of them all, although he never consciously forgot that Maggie would not have let him within shouting distance of such a table. Upon this table also stood his mother's jar of jelly.

The old women did not keep him waiting long. This was one more thing in favor of his hostess. Here was a woman of her word. Being made to wait was something he was inured to, but did not like. It was to be expected from grown-ups, toward a child. But, obviously, the very old woman who came leaning on the arm of her daughter-in-law, and carrying a cane in her free hand, had herself been waiting for her guest. She stopped short in front of him and gave him a long smiling look, without a word, as a contemporary might have done. Then she said,

"If he sits with his back to the light I won't be able to see his face. Put him there."

While she was being seated, with a difficult lowering of the limbs to a thick cushion, he changed his place. She propped her cane against the arm of the chair, and turned to consider him again. He, as frankly, looked at her.

She was old, so old that the bones seemed to push through the skin of her face. The skin, wrinkled, bleached and spotted, was of the colors of a winter leaf, and yet soft. The lips were pale, tending to a tone of purple—nothing so strong as purple, in truth, but his honest eyes reported to him the faint tinge of blue. He did not think it unpleasant. He knew so little of illness that it did not say to him at once, ah, a weakening heart. The mouth was a nice mouth, gentle and smiling. And if a strange sour smell had very faintly entered the room with her, it was overlaid by another scent, something associated in his mind with clean sheets and embroidered pillowcases.

Her hair, surprisingly darker than that of her daughter-in-law, was frizzed over her forehead. Stiff little disorderly strands escaped at the back of her neck, above her high, ruched collar. She wore a great many strings of beads, very interesting in their shapes and colors. She wore rings on the fingers of both hands. The sleeves of her white underwear—long underwear in late August!—showed at the wrists of her long sleeves. She kept her mouth closed when she smiled at him. When she spoke he had observed that she had all her teeth, and that they were very strong and even. Indeed, for teeth, she seemed better off than he was himself at that time, being then in the process of exchanging his milk teeth for some new incisors. All in all, he found nothing fearsome in her presence, unless there was a something behind her eyes, that knowledge of being almost ninety years old.

The daughter-in-law moved behind the tea-table and placed her hand inquiringly on the bright copper tea-kettle.

"It's tepid," she said. "Rachel brought it in too soon."

"That Rachel!" exclaimed the very old woman.

"We've never been able to convince her," said the daughter-in-law, "that tea ought to be made in the kitchen. She likes to put everything on the table at once. I'll take it all to the kitchen, Mother, and make it myself. But," she said, addressing the little boy, "you'd probably rather have a glass of milk, wouldn't you?"

"I have tea with my mother," he said. "Cambric tea."

"Good," she said. "I used to have muslin tea, when I was a child."

"Is it very different?" he asked.

"I should say that cambric was a cut above muslin," she replied, and went off, carrying the tea-pot in one hand, the copper kettle in the other.

The very old woman turned to the boy.

"That Rachel doesn't understand tea," she said, "but she makes very good cakes. Do you like cakes? So do I, and I like jelly. In fact, I'm *very* fond of jelly. Your mother knows that. Let's unwrap it."

He brought her the jar, and set it on her knees, and watched intently while she untied the pink ribbon with her extraordinarily small and bony fingers. She pushed the tissue paper away and admired the gift.

"Quince," she said, with satisfaction. "She knows I'm especially fond of quince. It's very good of her to remember that. Now put it on the table again."

He did as he was told, and returned to his chair. The sunlight glowing through the jelly was exactly the color of the sky at bedtime, when he looked out through the branches of the elm tree to the west. He leaned back in his chair, beginning to feel at ease with this very old woman, but his back could not reach the back of the chair while he sat with his knees bent at the edge. He did not feel quite enough at his ease to slide back in the chair with his legs straight before him, so he sat up straight again. His feet did not reach the floor.

"You wouldn't know," said the very old woman," that my husband planted the first quince trees in this town."

"We have a quince tree," he offered.

"My husband planted it. My husband built the house where you live. I am very old, you know. I came to this house as a bride. I can remember when there were only three houses on this street, and this was one of them. Yes, I am very old. And you are very young. We have that in common."

The logic of her remark escaped him, but the smile she gave him united them. They sat without speaking for a few minutes while he considered asking her whether she had ever seen an Indian. Perhaps she would not like to be thought as old as that. He rejected the idea. Then she said,

"I'm a great trial to my daughter, but she's very good to me. Ah, here she comes. Now we shall have our tea."

"The first cup for you, Mother?" asked the daughter-in-law.

"No, the first cup for our guest, for the cambric tea. I want mine strong to-day. Very strong."

"You know what the doctor said."

"A fig for what he said. If I'm not old enough now to have my tea as I like it, when shall I ever be?"

"Goodness only knows," said the other woman. To the boy, "There now. Plenty of cream and plenty of sugar. No, stay where you are—I'll bring it to you.

And a napkin on your knee. So. And there's a spoon. And remember it's hot.''

The room was so full of sunlight that it fell upon his lap as well as on the tea-table, and, caught in the bowl of the spoon, was reflected upward through the thin china. Even through the cloud of cream in the pale amber fluid it shone, and when he touched the spoon, it danced in the cloud.

He was content merely to hold this beautiful cup and saucer. He knew that the drink would be delicious. He waited politely, while the old woman prepared a cup for the very old woman, and carried it to her, as she had carried his cup to him. But as she turned back towards the table, the hands of the very old woman somehow lost control of cup and saucer. The cup tipped over in the saucer, the saucer tilted, and a great splash of hot tea fell upon her lap and spread down over her skirt. She gave a little cry of dismay. The daughter-in-law, seeing the accident, also cried out.

"Oh, Mother! On your best peau de soie! What a pity!"

The cry seemed to the child more sharp than perhaps it was. There merged with it, in his inward ear, the voice of Maggie, as she had said to him, "There's not a thing you touch that's safe!" And while the daughter-in-law knelt beside the older woman, sopping up the tea with a napkin, the voice went on in his head, relentless. "Sure, she's got the right to die. She's that old, there's not a drink she doesn't spill on herself. There's not a good cup in the house any longer. She couldn't be trusted with a good cup did one remain.''

He dared not move. He could not possibly have got out of the chair unassisted without capsizing his own cup of tea. He watched in misery, panic and sympathy while the mopping up took place. The daughter-in-law got up from her knees with difficulty, as short, stout people usually do. The very old woman murmured, over and over,

"I'm so ashamed, I'm so ashamed.''

Then the child summoned his courage and stood up to Maggie.

"I often spill things too,'' he said.

The daughter-in-law looked at him in surprise, as if she had forgotten his presence, and then at the soggy linen in her hand. She sighed.

"Well, so do I,'' she said, and laid the napkin on a corner of the tea tray. "Let me give you some more tea, Mother.''

"I break things, too,'' said the boy, firmly.

"Yes, yes, so do I,'' said his hostess.

The terror of Maggie's voice was silenced. Panic ebbed from the air. He took a long draft of warm sweetened milk, and comfort pervaded his small body, spreading from his stomach outward. He had a cake. The very old woman had a cake also, and licked her fingers afterwards. The daughter presiding over the tea-table also ate and drank, and appeared happy. A breeze sprang up outdoors, in the stillness of the afternoon, for an elm branch, swaying, made the sunlight flicker throughout the room. He was marvellously contented, and the more so because of the touch of peril earlier. He hooked a forefinger lovingly through the handle of his cup—smooth gold it was, and curving out below his finger in a little tail. It reminded him of something—the horn on the rear end of the caterpillar, that was it, the same curve, exactly.

He thought about the caterpillar, remembering it minutely, the embossed gold spots, the porcelain glossiness, its bulging segments, the tufts of white hairs. It had more than a little in common with the cup, for it was beautiful; but it was also ugly. The cup was truly beautiful, and it was more. It was a thing of civilization. It bestowed dignity upon him. To drink from it was an honor as well as a pleasure. The caterpillar was a funny little animal, with its own life to lead, eating leaves and crawling up and down in the dusk of the tomatoe vines. To the woman at the table he said, gravely,

"This is a breakable cup, isn't it?"

"It could hardly be more so," she replied.

"Maggie wouldn't let me touch it," he said. "But my mother says tea always tastes better from a breakable cup."

"Your mother is a woman after my own heart," said his hostess.

"Yes," said the very old woman happily. "My daughter would never serve me tea in anything but a breakable cup."